A Habit
of Death

Christopher Bryan

Diamond Press

A Habit of Death

Christopher Bryan

Printed in the United States of America.

The Diamond Press

Proctors Hall Road

Sewanee, Tennessee

For more information about this book, visit:

www.christopherbryanonline.com

Edition ISBNs

Trade Paperback 978-0-9853911-7-1

e-book 978-0-9853911-8-8

Library of Congress Cataloging-in-Publication data is available upon request.

First Edition 2015

This edition was prepared for printing by The Editorial Department

7650 E. Broadway, #308, Tucson, Arizona 85710

www.editorialdepartment.com

Cover design by Pete Garceau

Book design by Christopher Fisher

Diamond Press logo by Richard Posan for Two Ps

Photograph of Christopher Bryan by Wendy Elizabeth Bryan

In memoriam
Ellen Bradshaw Aitken
1961-2014

ΔΙΚΑΙΩΝ δὲ ψυχαὶ ἐν χειρὶ Θεοῦ, καὶ οὐ μὴ ἅψηται αὐτῶν βάσανος.

A HABIT OF DEATH

PROLOGUE

The Hospital Wing, Belmarsh Prison in South East London, 1ˢᵗ September 2013.

Superficially, being inside the three-story hospital wing of Belmarsh Prison in South East London was much like being in any other hospital. There were doctors and nurses. There were beds and charts, medicines and monitors, and all the usual paraphernalia of healing and sometimes death in the early decades of the twenty-first century. The difference from other hospitals was simply that this *was* a prison, and an adult male Category A prison at that.

In one of the wards on this particular September morning an old man lay dying. His sons and grandsons were gathered around him. But this was no ordinary old man. This was Jakov Morina, head of the Morina family. He and his had once been the aristocracy of London's criminal world and even now, confined in Belmarsh Prison at Her Majesty's pleasure, still they had some power in the world at large if they chose to exercise it.

The prison service had given permission for Jakov's sons and grandsons to be with him for his last moments. But security was strict, and they neither came to the ward nor would leave it without supervision.

The conversation was in Jakov's native Albanian, which his sons Armend and Pjeter understood perfectly, Armend's sons Jakov and Rnor understood somewhat, and the prison guards standing around them understood not at all. Normally the guards would have insisted on English, but in this moment of parting, as the old man lingered upon the threshold of death, someone had decreed that compassion prevail over security.

Jakov's voice was fragile, and his sons bent forward to hear him.

"You are the future of our family," he said. "You must uphold the credit of our house. To you Armend as my eldest falls the chief responsibility."

"I understand, Father."

"You must communicate with my grandson Shpend. Tell him that although he is out in the world, still I want him to stay close to you all. That is my command. Keep him in your fold."

"We will, Father."

"He must continue to watch over my granddaughter Ariana, as must you all, even from here. She has chosen her own path. It is not our path, but it is an honourable path, and she must be protected while she is upon it. That is my command. Is that understood?"

"Yes, Father. We understand."

There was silence for several minutes, and when the old man spoke again his voice was scarcely more than a whisper.

"I am tired. You must leave me now. I will sleep. I believe that I will not wake again, not in this life. And what some other life may hold for me I do not know. I would give much to see my beloved wife again, my own Ariana, the companion of my bed and the light of my hearth. But who knows? I have done much evil in the world and only a little good. But you my sons and grandsons, all of you, uphold the honour of our house."

The old man held out his hand, which was white, veined, and trembling.

One by one, his sons and grandsons came to him where he lay in the hospital bed, bent over his hand and kissed it.

They left in silence, and were escorted back to their cells.

Jakov Morina slept.

And did not wake again.

ONE

Edgestow, Devon. Tuesday, 5ᵗʰ November 2013.
Just after 10:30 p.m.

St. Boniface Abbey near Edgestow in the county of Devon was a quiet place. There, amid Tudor brick and medieval stone, the good sisters of St. Boniface had prayed and sung for more than a hundred and fifty years. They had also busied themselves with visiting the sick, the lonely, and the poor, looking after flowers, fruit trees, and vegetables, and taking care of their chickens. Yet even with all this activity, the abbey remained tranquil.

Except for the fifth of November — Bonfire Night! Not, of course, that the sisters set off any fireworks or lit any bonfires. The sisters sang Compline as usual. But even the walls of the abbey could not shut out the bright lights and colors that filled the sky over Edgestow. So after Compline Sister Barbara, who was sacristan that week, put out the candles and made sure everything was in its place, and then the sisters, being sensible as well as good, sat outside their chapel in cool darkness and enjoyed the last twenty minutes or so of the spectacle, only when it was over rising and preparing to begin the Great Silence.

But then Dismas the dog, having sat peacefully enough through the fireworks, became unhappy. He got to his feet and grumbled, pointing towards the orchard.

"Perhaps he smells a fox," Mother Evelyn said. "Are the chickens locked up?"

"Safe and sound. I saw to it before Compline," Sister Athanasius said.

"Good."

"I think," Sister Barbara said, "I'll begin Silence with my walk in the orchard for a few minutes, if I may."

"Of course," Mother Evelyn said. Sister Barbara had for years liked to walk alone with her Lord for a few minutes in the orchard after Compline. "We'll leave the door on the latch for you as usual. Try not to frighten the fox, dear!"

"I'll try not to, Mother."

"I'll take Dismas with us, as he's no doubt itching to bully it! He doesn't seem to understand that foxes too have a right to exist."

"Just so long as they don't eat our chickens, who also have a right to exist!" Sister Athanasius said.

Mother Evelyn smiled.

So the sisters bade each other soft good nights, a still grumbling Dismas was put on his lead and led away, and Sister Barbara folded her hands into her habit and walked slowly towards the orchard.

The Great Silence began.

Two

The digital alarm clock beside the bed sounded its call, piercing and peremptory. From beneath the duvet Detective Chief Inspector Cecilia Anna Maria Cavaliere of the Exeter CID reached out a finger, equally peremptory, and shut it up.

It was dark outside—today the sun would not rise until three minutes past seven—but already faint sounds came from the kitchen downstairs. Friendly sounds, cooking sounds, mingled with chat from Radio 2 and the aroma of baking bread.

Cecilia took a deep, pleasurable breath, and stretched luxuriously.

The iPhone next to the clock glowed and barked.

She sat up and peered at it.

It was her husband Michael, who was an Anglican parish priest and rector of St. Mary's Church in Exeter. They were apart at the moment because the arrival in Edgestow some months earlier of the United Nations Institute for Technological Experimentation and Development ("U.N.I.T.E.D.") had created a need for more formidable police presence in the little town. Since late August Cecilia and a group of officers under her direction had been providing that presence. Their assignment was to end in just over two weeks, when the new Edgestow Police Station with its own officers under their own superintendent was to be declared open for business.

"Hello, Italian police lady," Michael said.

"Hello, vicar that's married to her."

"I miss you."

"So do I. That is—I mean, *I* miss *you*."

"Did I wake you?"

"You didn't exactly *wake* me. I was gradually surfacing."

"I wanted to catch you before you started work."

"Well you managed that all right."

"Here's the thing—there's a chap in your papa's department who can let us have two free tickets, orchestra stalls, for *Les Vêpres siciliennes* at Covent Garden on the fifteenth. Only Papa has to tell him if we want them when he goes in this morning for his eight o'clock class." Papa was professor of classics at the university. "So would you be up for that? Papa says he and Mama will look after Rachel."

"Oh, *yes!*" She'd been wanting to go to the Verdi centenary production so badly she could taste it. "I'm sure it'll be fine, but hang on!"

She skipped across the room, shivering slightly, for it was cold after the warmth of her duvet, and looked in her diary.

"It *is* yes! I'd love to."

"Good! I'll tell Papa. That's for the fifteenth."

"Got it! Darling, I do love you but can I go now? I'm freezing!"

"Yes. I love you, too."

"You'd better! 'Bye."

THREE

Mother Evelyn came down the stairs and saw that the front door was already unlatched. Good! Sister Barbara, who was on sacristy duty that week, was obviously on the job. She would already be in chapel, making ready for Prime.

Mother Evelyn turned on the hall lights, collected an electric torch from the basket on the stand by the door—she would need it, for the sun would not be up for another hour or so yet—and went out.

It was cold, but she didn't mind. She loved walking to chapel in the dark. Indeed, she loved worshipping there when it was dark. At such times she felt close to God and (let's be honest, she told herself) she also felt *very* romantic and medieval. All those lovely candles!

Still, she was also glad of the powerful LED torch. Romantic and medieval were fine in their way, but there was a place for twenty-first century technology, too. She certainly wouldn't want to go to a medieval dentist!

She rounded the corner of the main building to face the chapel.

And stopped.

It was in total darkness, still and silent.

Sister Barbara must be only moments ahead of her.

She walked slowly, waiting for the lights to go on.

Nothing moved. Nothing changed.

A gust of cold wind rattled some bushes and died away.

Silence.

And still no lights.

So she'd been wrong. Sister Barbara was *not* on the job.

Had she overslept?

But then, the front door had been unlatched.

So did Sister Barbara forget to latch it when she came in last night and then oversleep? *One* such failure to fulfill an obligation was unlike her, let alone two.

Or —

Mother Evelyn stopped.

Had she not come in at all?

Mother Evelyn turned and with now more urgent step took another path, away from the chapel towards the orchard. In a moment the sharp beam of her torch was picking out west country apple trees in their neat, orderly rows: sensible Lane Prince Albert at this end, its fruit perfect for cooking; then further on trees of a more romantic bent: Adams Pearman, Beauty of Bath, and her personal favorite, Cornish Gilli —

Her heart jumped. On the grass between the trees the light from her torch was picking up something reflective: two circles that shone back at her.

A pair of glasses.

Sister Barbara wore glasses.

And now, beyond the yellow circles, something else.

Something that as she stared at it flapped and shifted in the wind.

Oh dear God.

She forced herself to go on, now sure that in a moment she would know what she did not wish to know.

She gazed down.

Sister Barbara lay face up, her features white in the beam of the torch. Mother Evelyn knelt and felt for a pulse in skin that was icy cold. But it was as she had known in her heart it would be.

Sister Barbara had no pulse.

FOUR

Cecilia Cavaliere's lodgings. The kitchen. 6:30 a.m.

The aroma of bread now had competition. Coffee and frying bacon were inviting attention. It was a close-run thing, but the coffee was nearer and for the moment it won.

"Last night seems to have passed off well enough," Cecilia said some minutes later, setting down her cup.

The fact was, wherever she was, as a police officer she was always glad to get Guy Fawkes Night over with, relieved if it passed off without major injury or incident. But even for her, last night in Edgestow had actually been rather pleasant. It had been for the most part a local crowd, evidently in good spirits, happy and enjoying itself, and all in an entirely civilized manner. Somewhat to her surprise she'd found herself in bed by a little after one, with no problems she was aware of and nothing of note reported by any of her officers.

"Yes, ma'am," Mrs. Abney said. "A lovely bonfire, and very nice fireworks, I thought. Would you like another cup?"

"I would, Mrs. Abney. Excellent, as always!"

"Thank you, ma'am. We've got the right water for it. I always say you can't make good coffee if you don't have the right water for it, no matter how hard you try."

"That's true, Mrs. Abney. Still, it's also a fact that you use *excellent* beans."

"That's right, ma'am. Kenya Double A. Mr. Abney always liked Kenya Double A. Wouldn't have anything else in the house if he could avoid it."

"Well, using good beans and grinding them by hand has something to do with the good coffee too, I think!"

"Thank you, ma'am."

There was a suitably reverent pause while Cecilia drank some of her second Americano.

"Going back to last night," she said, "I gather Edgestow always has a sort of town party on Bonfire Night? These days in Exeter they seem to make more of Halloween."

Mrs. Abney nodded. "All those nasty witch costumes and skeletons and things! There's more money in it for the shops I expect, that's why they push it. But Edgestow does seem to have stuck with Guy Fawkes, at least for now."

"It was nice they invited the young men from Eglītis."

Eglītis was the Latvian security firm employed by U.N.I.T.E.D. The Institute had been involved in major scandal some ten weeks earlier, leading Cecilia and her colleagues to arrest its director and a number of its other personnel on a range of charges including murder and criminal conspiracy. As if all that were not enough, a local earthquake had then brought down a considerable part of the main administration building, whose designers had, it transpired, ignored a number of rather precise limitations and recommendations in the geological survey that preceded its construction.

In the weeks following these disasters, however, a new director had been appointed—a Yorkshireman from the Dales who was also an environmentalist, and whose first remark on seeing the place had been, apparently, "For God's sake, let's plant some trees!"

Under his leadership, it seemed, things were beginning to recover.

"I got the impression quite a few of the Eglītis men came," Cecilia said.

"That was Mr. Dawson's idea." Mr. Dawson was the Methodist minister. "They seem to be nice lads, now you've got rid of those awkward ones. I think one of them is getting sweet on our Jennifer in The Great Western."

"Is he now!"

Cecilia's mobile rang.

"DCI Cavaliere," she said.

"Sergeant Wyatt, ma'am."

"Good morning, Sergeant. What's up?"

"Ma'am, Doctor Musgrave has been on the phone. She's out at the abbey—St. Boniface Abbey. You know it?"

"On the left as you come in from St. Anne's, big stone wall and the gate's alongside the road?"

"That's right ma'am. Well it seems one of the sisters died last night. They found her lying in the orchard this morning. They thought she'd just keeled over—she had a heart condition they knew about—but Doctor Musgrave's seen the body and she says there's a difficulty. She wants the police to look at it."

"Oh." Susan Musgrave was a local GP. In the few dealings they'd had with each other over the last ten or so weeks she'd impressed Cecilia as a sensible, competent physician who wouldn't be making a fuss about nothing. "All right. Then I suppose I'm on my way. Call DS Jones, tell her there's a possibly suspicious death, and ask her to meet me there, will you? Do we have anyone else near the abbey?"

"I knew Wilkins would be passing on his way in from his digs, so I've already told him to look in and hold the fort until you get there."

"Excellent, Sergeant."

She put the phone back into her bag, looked at Mrs. Abney, and shook her head.

"And I was just congratulating myself we'd got through Guy Fawkes' night without incident."

"Never mind, ma'am," Mrs. Abney said. "I'll make you a nice bacon and egg sandwich and you can eat it in the car."

FIVE

It had been dark when Cecilia set off from Mrs. Abney's, but by the time she reached the abbey there were glimmers of light in the eastern sky. It was the first time she'd seen the big double gates open. She pulled into the drive. A blue and yellow police panda car, its lights still on, was parked in front of the main building, which was Tudor brick and stone, with lights on in a number of rooms. There were late chrysanthemums blooming in stone urns under the shelter of the porch by the main door.

Beside the panda car stood PC Wilkins and a sister in a black habit.

They both looked up as Cecilia's tires sounded on the gravel. The constable looked relieved and Cecilia swallowed a smile. Doubtless the young man was not used to dealing with religious.

She pulled around a grass circle with a statue in the middle—a bearded man wearing a mitre and carrying an axe, presumably St. Boniface—and brought the Volvo to a stop behind the panda.

The sister turned to her as she got out.

"Hello," she said. "I take it you're also from the police?" Her face was serious.

Cecilia produced her warrant card.

"I'm Detective Chief Inspector Cavaliere, Exeter CID," she said. "I understand you have some rather bad news."

"I'm afraid we have, Chief Inspector. Forgive me—I'm forgetting my manners. I'm Sister Francis. Please, follow me. I'll take you there at once."

A little card on the door said "Sister Barbara."

The room was simply furnished and without ornament save for a crucifix, a portrait of the Blessed Virgin, and a lit candle. But it was pleasantly proportioned and did not look uncomfortable. Did one call it a cell?

Sister Barbara—Cecilia presumed it must be Sister Barbara— lay on the bed, a slight figure, prone, in her habit, her features calm in the peace of death. Doctor Susan Musgrove stood beside her, looking slightly defensive, and there was another nun in the room: small, slim, and bespectacled.

"Good morning, Susan," Cecilia said to the doctor, then turned to the nun. "I'm Detective Chief Inspector Cavaliere from Exeter CID."

"And I'm Mother Evelyn. I'm the prioress."

Cecilia nodded. "Would you like to tell me what's happened, Mother?"

"I found Sister Barbara in the orchard this morning. I realized she was dead—she was stone cold and there wasn't any pulse—and we assumed she'd had a heart attack last night while she was walking there. She had a heart condition, and Doctor Musgrave has been attending her for it for some time."

She looked at the doctor, who nodded.

"So we brought her in and laid her on her bed while we called the doctor—it didn't seem right to leave her out there in the orchard. We were going to take her to the chapel later, and begin arrangements for her funeral. But now Doctor Musgrave says she must notify the coroner."

"Doctor?"

"I'm really very sorry." Susan Musgrove turned to the figure on the bed. "Sister Barbara *did* have a heart condition, it's true. But as you can see, her skin is slightly purple and there are petechiae round her nose and mouth."

Cecilia drew in her breath sharply.

Petechiae—small spots, the signs of minor hemorrhaging caused by broken capillary blood vessels. She could already see where this was going.

"Then when I examined her," the doctor continued, "I found what look like marks of severe bruising on her neck. What this means, I'm afraid, is there'll have to be an autopsy. I don't think Sister Barbara did die of a heart attack. I think she was strangled."

SIX

St. Boniface Abbey, a few minutes later.

Cecilia and PC Wilkins walked out onto the porch. The eastern sky was by now awash with light.

"Constable," Cecilia said, "secure the orchard as a probable crime scene, will you? It's possible the autopsy will decide Doctor Musgrave was wrong, but I doubt it. And if she's right, we've got a murder on our hands."

"Yes, ma'am. Though from what the other lady said, it sounds though as if they've already screwed it up—as a crime scene I mean."

Cecilia nodded.

"I'm afraid so," she said. "Still, the scene-of-crime lot are pretty hot, so with luck they'll salvage something."

As PC Wilkins left for the orchard, there was a creaking of tires on gravel and a white Ford Fiesta pulled into the yard. This was Detective Sergeant Verity Jones looking, as was her habit even at this time of the morning, as though she had stepped from the pages of a fashion magazine. Cecilia had once been somewhat disconcerted by this almost unremitting sartorial perfection on the part of her junior colleague, secretly thinking of her as "little Miss Perfect." But she was long past that, having found in Verity over several years a faithful friend—a friend who had, moreover, a double first in *literae humaniores*, a mind like a steel trap, and no fear whatsoever of hard work.

"DS Jones," she said. "Good. Short story for now—it looks as if one of the sisters has been murdered. Apparently they've all been together since the body was found, so we might as well begin by interviewing them together. Then we can talk to them separately later. Can you find Mother Evelyn—I think she's still in the victim's room, second floor—and arrange that with her? She also said there's a big old refectory that we can set up as an incident room. Sort that out with her too, would you? Meanwhile I'll get on to Exeter. We're going to need an MCIT—SOCO's, forensics, more uniform, the lot."

Verity nodded.

"On it, ma'am."

"And there's going to be a lot of interviewing to do. We can involve uniform in some of that. Wilkins and Jarman have both put in for detective. This will be a good chance for them to get some more experience."

The community gathered in what was called the library at about 9:30 a.m., as soon as they had finished saying Morning Prayer. It was a tall, handsome room with large windows and many bookshelves, but few books.

Mother Evelyn noticed Cecilia's reaction. "We had quite a valuable collection once but we had to sell it some years ago to pay the bills. Anglican sisterhoods aren't very profitable these days!"

In addition to Dismas the dog (brown, medium-sized, of indeterminate ancestry and not a suspect) there were five women seated facing the two police officers. Mother Evelyn the prioress, who appeared to be in her middle years. Sister Agnes, also in her middle years. Sister Francis and Sister Athanasius, who seemed quite elderly. And Sister Chiara, who was a relatively young woman—about DS Jones's age, Cecilia judged—and rather beautiful.

"Let me begin," Cecilia said, "by saying how sorry I am for your loss and distressed that I must intrude on your grief. But there are circumstances surrounding Sister Barbara's death that mean there will have to be a police investigation, and for the present, at least, I will have to lead it."

Mother Evelyn smiled gently.

"Detective Chief Inspector," she said, "we also are women under authority."

Cecilia nodded.

"Thank you," she said. "Not everyone has such a sensible attitude."

She paused. "So, our first question has to be, who last saw Sister Barbara alive?"

The five looked at each other.

"I think all of us together," Mother Evelyn said. "We were all at Compline—that's the last service of the day."

Cecilia smiled and nodded.

"Normally Compline at ten o'clock begins the Great Silence, which lasts until six o'clock in the morning, but because last night was Guy Fawkes' Night, we stayed up and watched the fireworks. Then when they were over—about eleven, I should think—we began the Silence and went to bed. Sister Barbara quite often liked to walk alone for a while in the orchard at the beginning of Silence and had permission to do that. So we'd leave the door unlatched for her, knowing she'd come in when she was ready and lock up. And that was what we did."

She looked at the others, who nodded.

"That's about it," Sister Agnes said.

"But then when I got up this morning for Prime," Evelyn continued, "the door was still unlatched and the chapel was empty and there was no Sister Barbara. So I went to the orchard and … and … there she was."

Sister Chiara, who was seated next to her, took her hand.

There was a moment of silence.

"So then?" Cecilia said gently.

"So then Sister Agnes and Sister Chiara arrived."

Cecilia looked at them.

"We'd come over at more or less the same time as each other for Prime," Sister Agnes said. "It was still dark. We saw there was no light in the chapel and realized something must be wrong. Then Sister Francis and Sister Athanasius arrived, and just about then Chiara noticed a light in the orchard." She hesitated. "You'll understand we'd decided by now that we had to break Silence at least until we knew what was going on."

She looked at Mother Evelyn.

"Of course," she said. "You were quite right."

"So then we all went to the orchard and found Mother Evelyn—and Sister Barbara," Sister Agnes said.

The others nodded.

"Sister Barbara was stone cold and I couldn't find a pulse," Mother Evelyn said. "So I was sure she was dead. But I must admit I didn't think about murder, I just assumed it was a heart attack. I suppose we all did. We all knew about her condition."

She looked at the others and again they nodded.

"Anyway we carried her to her room and telephoned Doctor Musgrave and she, bless her, came round straight away, and for the rest, well, you know what the doctor said."

"Thank you," Cecilia said. "That's very clear and helpful. Next, we'd like to learn what we can about Sister Barbara herself. Her life before she took her vows. It may be helpful if—oh, thank you!"

As Cecilia was speaking Mother Evelyn had turned and taken from the table behind her a brown manila folder, which she now handed over. "Sister Barbara, OSB" was printed on it in large letters.

"I thought you'd want some background," Sister Evelyn said. "And that's her file. She entered the order in 1993 and was professed in 1998. Before that she was in banking—and was rather high-powered, I think. But it's in the file."

Cecilia opened it. On top of the papers was a photograph: head and shoulders of a woman with glasses and strong, rather striking features, wearing a religious habit. Cecilia gazed at it for a moment, and then looked up.

"I'm sure this will be helpful. Thank you."

She closed the folder and handed it to Verity.

"Next—are there any regular visitors to the abbey that we ought to know about? People who come in to work, to do your gardens and cooking and so on?"

"We do all our housework ourselves," Mother Evelyn said, "and we also tend the garden."

"That's a lot."

"The order used to be much larger than it is now. But we manage, as you see. And there are people who come in and help. There's Dick Posan, who comes to us two or three times a week and works on the gardens and fixes things in the house. Or he comes more times if we need. He's marvelous."

"He's our man what can and what does," Sister Agnes said. "And on the very rare occasions when he *can't*, he invariably knows someone else what can and will and won't charge too much!"

There were smiles and nods.

"Then there's Jennifer," Sister Francis said. "Jennifer Pettigrew. She takes our spare produce to the market for us. We make a bit of money that way. And it's all organic."

"That's Jennifer from The Great Western? The landlord's daughter?"

"Yes."

"Good. Anyone else?"

A pause.

"Sister Barbara did have a visitor on Friday before last," Chiara said.

"Did she?"

"Midmorning. I was vacuuming the hall and she came down to meet him and took him to the office. She was our treasurer, you know."

The former banker as treasurer: that made sense.

"Did you hear what they were talking about?"

"No. I was vacuuming! But they did seem quite friendly with each other. They were laughing about something."

"Does anyone know who this man was? Did Sister Barbara say anything to anyone about him?"

There were blank looks and headshakes all round.

"Do you remember what he looked like?"

"About five foot nine," Sister Chiara said. "Average build. Rimless glasses. Balding. Clean-shaven. Dark blue suit. But I'm afraid I didn't really look at him much. I was more concerned with the hall carpet."

Cecilia exchanged a look with Verity, and smiled.

"I dare say you were," she said, "but that's still not at all a bad description."

"I did see his car when I went out to empty the bag," Chiara added. "At least, I suppose it was his car."

"And?"

"It was an Audi, A4 sedan, metallic silver." She hesitated. "The age identifier was 62—that's late 2012 or early 2013, I believe."

Cecilia raised an eyebrow.

"She can't help it," Sister Agnes said. "She just likes cars."

"I'm glad she does! Thank you, Sister. That's quite a lot to go on."

There was a pause.

"Oh," Mother Evelyn said, "and then there's the chaplain."

"Who is a pompous ass," Sister Agnes said.

Sister Chiara and Sister Athanasius giggled.

"Sisters!" Mother Evelyn said in a tone of rebuke that was not, to tell the truth, entirely convincing. "He is priest of the church and needs our prayers."

"Yes, Mother, he certainly does!" Sister Agnes said.

Again Chiara and Athanasius giggled.

Cecilia swallowed a smile. She had a sense that for a moment the shadow lifted from the group. She was seeing them as they were when they were not in the shock of grief, able to be frank and playful with each another.

She looked at Mother Evelyn.

"And who is this chaplain?" she asked.

"Father Carlton. He's the rector of St. Anne's. He comes in on Sundays and major festivals to say Mass, and he hears our confessions."

"Sounds like harmless enough occupation for a turbulent priest," Verity said unexpectedly, looking up from her notebook.

Sister Agnes and Sister Chiara laughed.

Silence. The shadow returned.

"And that's it, as far as regular visitors are concerned?"

The sisters looked each other, and nodded.

"I think so," Mother Evelyn said.

"So, finally for the moment, do any of you have any ideas or thoughts as to who might have killed Sister Barbara?"

"No, Chief Inspector."

"No."

"Not the slightest."

"No."

"No."

She had looked at each of them in turn, but nobody had evaded the question.

SEVEN

After their interview with the community Cecilia and Verity sat together with cups of tea in the newly commissioned incident room and read through the file on Sister Barbara. It didn't take long. There was a note of her name before she joined the order—Alice Hermione Walker. There were the names of schools she'd attended in London and dates when she'd attended them. There were brief records of her working at the London headquarters of the Midland Bank in Poultry.

"Poultry?" Verity said, looking up.

"It's a street between Cheapside and Bank Junction—heart of the financial district. But they used to sell chickens there until fifteen-something."

"And just exactly how is a simple little girl from the Welsh mountains supposed to know *that*?"

Cecilia shook her head. "Verity, the gaps in your basic education continue to appall me. Only the other day you admitted you didn't *even* know that a number 36 bus goes from Paddington Station to Hyde Park Corner!"

Verity chuckled, and went back to her reading.

There were notes about Sister Barbara's attendance and confirmation at a London Church — St. James, Sussex Gardens. And there was her acceptance into the Order of St. Boniface.

"It's bare bones," Cecilia said when they had finished. "There's no flesh." She picked up the photograph and gazed at it. "We need to know about the *woman*. This doesn't even tell us who her family were, or where she came from."

Verity replaced the last sheet she had looked at, and nodded.

"I think maybe Joseph can help there. Shall I ask him to start digging? See what he can find out about her?"

"That would be good."

Joseph Stirrup was their invariable first source for research and information — a Bahamian computer genius who was also Verity's newly appointed fiancé. Until little over a year ago he'd been confined to a wheel chair, but an operation followed by extensive physiotherapy had achieved major success, and now he was able to get about quite well with a stick.

Cecilia sat back in her chair and considered.

"So what did you think of the community?" she said. "Theoretically, I suppose, one of them could have done it. Since they split up after the fireworks and went separately to their rooms, and since they all knew where Sister Barbara was, that means every one of them had opportunity. And since she was fragile with a weak heart, probably any one of them could have managed it physically."

"Motive?" Verity said.

"Frustrated celibate spinsters endlessly at close quarters? Petty rivalries and jealousies in a hothouse of repressed emotions? No doubt repressed sexual tensions too? So finally someone gives way, there's an explosion of previously suppressed anger, and a killing."

Verity nodded.

"With Guy Fawkes night as the final catalyst," she said. "All those explosions and lights, a hint of violence in the air, even the faint smell of cordite. For one of the sisters it is finally too much. She asks herself why should Sister Barbara be the one who has the privilege of staying up late and walking in the orchard? And finally she decides — let her pay for that privilege with her life!"

"So all we have to do is find out which of the sisters it was who lost her cool, and arrest her?"

"Exactly. A walk in the park."

There was a pause.

"So do we think that's the way it was?" Cecilia asked.

Verity gave faint smile.

"It probably would if this were an episode of *Midsomer Murders*."

Cecilia laughed. They'd been discussing the television series a few days earlier, and both commented on the fact that whenever anyone religious appeared in the plot they invariably turned out to be either mad or homicidal or both. They'd also observed that given the number of episodes and the average number of murders in each one, the homicide rate in the pretty little rural villages of the county of Midsomer had to be rather higher than that of Los Angeles.

"For what my impression's worth," Verity said, "I thought the sisters' relationships seemed pretty good. They wouldn't be human if they didn't have disagreements but I don't sense any real tensions among them. When Agnes was rude about the chaplain, they all thought it was really funny."

Cecilia chuckled. "With her the naughty one, and the rest of them enjoying it even though elder sister Mother Evelyn feels it's up to her to be shocked and responsible!"

"Of course they may just be putting on a show for our benefit. But if they are, then they are five very competent actors. Which I somehow doubt."

"I agree," Cecilia said. "Still, we can't rule anyone out yet." She sighed.

"Michael led a retreat for them just before Easter. I wonder what he made of them."

"Couldn't you ask him?" Verity said.

Could she?

Generally she enjoyed discussing her cases with Michael — something she'd done even before they started going out together. She could think of a couple of breakthroughs she'd had as a direct result of his coming back at her about something she'd told him. But those were cases in which he wasn't personally involved. In this instance, the fact that he'd worked with the sisters was a reason why his insights might be especially valuable — but also a reason why he might not be able to share them. And if it were a matter of something he'd heard in the confessional, of course there would be no way he could divulge it.

She sighed.

"I suppose there's no harm in asking," she said finally.

Michael was clearly distressed when Cecilia phoned and told him of Sister Barbara's death.

"Dear God, how awful! Such a gentle, gracious group! That someone would do something like this to one of them!"

"Do you remember Sister Barbara?" Cecilia asked.

"Certainly I remember her. She came to talk to me."

"Look — I don't want to put you on the spot and I know there may be things you just can't tell me. But do you have *any* thoughts or impressions you could talk about? We're scrabbling in the dark at the moment, and anything might help."

He paused for a few seconds.

"Well," he said, "Sister Barbara didn't come to me for confession, so we're all right there. And after what's happened, I hardly think she's likely to mind my telling you what we talked about if it might help catch her killer. It's not as if it was anything particularly embarrassing or awful. She wanted to talk theology. To be precise, she wanted to talk about forgiveness."

"Forgiveness?"

"She said, what if someone had committed sins against the Holy Spirit—the kind of sin the Bible says can't be forgiven?"

"And what did you say?"

"Nothing very profound or original, I'm afraid! I gave her the standard answer. There are no limits to God's mercy. The sin against the Holy Spirit is *refusing* God's mercy—in other words, refusing forgiveness, refusing to repent. And that's a sin that can't be forgiven for the simple reason that even God can't—or, at least, *won't*—force on us something that we refuse to take."

"And?"

"She said the sins she was talking about were nothing so subtle as that. She just meant ordinary human evil and wickedness. But that did include some things so terrible it seemed ludicrous to imagine their being forgiven."

"And you said?"

"I said, ludicrous to us, perhaps, but not to God. There's no sin that can't be forgiven if we're sorry for it. That's what God sent his Son for—to save sinners."

"Do you think she believed you?"

"I think perhaps she did. Sometimes—just occasionally—one is graced to say the right thing. Sister Barbara seemed to need that simple, evangelical declaration. I think maybe she'd been talking to a spiritual director or a confessor who wasn't helpful. And to be honest I wasn't even sure whether it was her own sins she was talking about or someone else's. I'm still not. Perhaps I should have pressed her on that. I'm afraid I didn't. I just let her lead the conversation where she seemed to want to go."

EIGHT

Exeter. St. Mary's Rectory. Michael's study. A few minutes later.

"Were you talking to Mummy on the phone?" three-year-old daughter Rachel said when Michael had replaced the handset.

"Yes, sweetheart."

"When will Mummy be home?"

"Well she was just with us for her weekend off, wasn't she? So she most likely won't be back before the end of next week. But then she'll be home for good. Her time working in Edgestow will be over."

Or would it? What about the murder? Could Sister Barbara's death mean that Cecilia would have to stay longer in Edgestow than had been planned? Damn.

Oh dear Lord, listen to him! It sounded as if he was getting annoyed with the poor woman for being murdered because her death might inconvenience him. How terribly inconsiderate of her!

Anyway, Cecilia hadn't said anything about having to stay longer in Edgestow.

So best cross that bridge if they came to it—and hope they didn't.

"I like it when Mummy's home," Rachel said.

Had she read his thoughts?

"So do I, sweetheart."

"I love Granny and Grandpa, too."

"Of course you do."

"And Figaro."

Figaro, on the rug by the hearth, thumped his tail.

"Yes."

"And Felix and Marlene."

Michael's cats Felix and Marlene, in a sleeping heap on what seemed somehow over the last few weeks, without any warrant from anyone, to have become "their" armchair, did not move at all.

"Yes, sweetheart."

"And Tocco and Pu."

Tocco and Pu were Mama's and Papa's dogs.

"Absolutely, sweetheart."

"And I like it best when we're all together."

"So do I."

"I liked it when we all went to Sam … Sam … to that field and had the chicken legs and things."

He smiled.

"Yes, wasn't that nice."

On the previous Saturday, while Cecilia was home for the weekend, it had been chilly but fine and sunny. So the whole family apart from Felix and Marlene — that is to say, Cecilia's mama and papa, Cecilia and Michael, daughter Rachel, and the three dogs Figaro, Tocco, and Pu — had gone to Salmon Pool Meadow for a winter picnic. They'd taken with them cold chicken legs and paninis stuffed with mozzarella and prosciutto, together with a bottle of cabernet sauvignon and a flask of hot coffee for the grown-ups and orange juice for Rachel. They'd had the whole place to themselves, including the two picnic tables, presumably because, as Cecilia observed, no one else in Exeter was insane enough on a freezing cold day to eat *al fresco* when they had a perfectly good house to eat in.

"Much though we love England," Papa said, more philosophically, "it would be hard to pretend that we came here for the climate."

"Oh, I don't know," Mama said. "It gives you a lovely excuse to have bacon and eggs for *prima collazione.*"

Michael nodded. Overall, Cecilia's mama spoke English well. But "breakfast" was a word that for some reason she had never adopted.

Rachel, armed with the zest, stamina, and chill-resistance of a three-year-old, and Figaro, Tocco, and Pu, with the built-in benefit of hairy insulation, rushed about wildly and happily together for most of the two hours they were there, apart from fifteen minutes or so when Cecilia insisted that Rachel sit with the rest of the family and eat—a ritual in which the three dogs were, of course, happy to assist.

In the end, however, it was Cecilia (wearing more than any of them—two sweaters, lined gloves, a woolly hat, and a thick coat) who said, "I'm sorry to be a pain and I absolutely adore this particular form of English insanity, but I'm freezing. Can we go home now, please?"

This sign of weakness on her part was, if truth be told, actually a source of mild satisfaction to Michael, who reckoned himself in most matters physical to be a complete wimp in comparison with his wife. Cecilia could swim, it appeared to him, forever (he was exhausted after a width of the baths), she could vault a four-foot fence without thinking about it (he'd seen her do it), and in a fair fight with her he reckoned he'd be lucky if he lasted fifteen seconds.

But he could, apparently, stand the cold better than she.

"You come of a hardy northern race," she said as they

piled into the car. "I, by contrast, if I am to flourish, need lots of beakers full of the warm South, the true, the blushful hippocrene."

"Cos'è ippocrene?" Rachel asked as they started off, speaking to her mother in Italian as she always did.

Cecilia looked around at them.

"I must admit I haven't the slightest idea," she said. "What *is* hippocrene? All I know is, Keats liked beakers of it, warm, true, and blushful. Just at the moment I rather think it was the 'warm' part that appealed to me."

Papa, jammed into the back with Mama and Rachel and three dogs, answered his granddaughter directly.

"Nella mitologia greca," he said, "Ippocrene era la fonte sacra alle Muse sull'Elicona, fatta sprizzare dal cavallo alato Pegaso con un colpo di zampa. L'espressione 'abbeverarsi alla fonte d'Ippocrene' venne a significare coltivar la poesia."

"Oh," Rachel said, in what could have been English or Italian.

There followed a longer than usual silence, during which she appeared to be digesting all this information about the sacred spring Hippocrene on Mount Helicon, and how it had been created by a blow from the hoof of Pegasus the winged horse.

Finally, she said, "Grazie."

Papa nodded.

"Prego," he said politely.

Michael hid a smile.

"There is a such a thing," he reflected as he took advantage of a lull in the traffic and pulled left from Salmon Pool Lane onto the Topsham Road, "as being told rather more when you've asked a question than you really wanted to know. Perhaps it's just as well to learn that sobering fact fairly early in life!"

"That was absolutely lovely," Cecilia said when they got home. And having taken Rachel upstairs for her nap, then took herself off to bed where she remained under a duvet and several blankets until teatime.

"It was good, that day with the chicken legs and things, but Mummy doesn't like being cold, does she?" Rachel said.

"She certainly doesn't."

"We'll have to pick a warm day next time. Then Mummy won't get cold."

"That's right, sweetheart. Let's do that."

"Mummy only came with us because she knew *we* wanted to go. She'd like to have stayed at home and not been cold."

"That's right, sweet—!" He stared at his daughter for a moment, then—

"Rachel, you are a genius!"

"What's a genius?"

He bent and kissed her.

"Someone who is *very* clever. And now I need to phone Mummy again."

NINE

St. Boniface Abbey, a few minutes later.

Cecilia's mobile rang. It was Michael.

"Cecilia, do you have another minute? I've remembered something else about my conversation with Sister Barbara. To tell you the truth, I can't think why I forgot it earlier. Anyway, something Rachel said made me think of it."

Cecilia heard herself make what Michael sometimes called her "mother confessor's encouraging little 'hmmm?' noise," and waited.

"Right at the start of our conversation, Sister Barbara said, 'What if your family had persuaded you to do terrible things?'"

"Really? And what then?"

"Then she got onto the questions I told you about — sin against the Holy Spirit and whether some sins couldn't be forgiven."

"And you didn't ask her about her family?"

"As I told you — I just let her lead the conversation where she seemed to want to go. She seemed to me to be a strong, self-aware woman who knew her own needs. But perhaps I was wrong. I often am."

Cecilia smiled and shook her head. No, she thought. In fact, you're usually right.

"Anyway," Michael continued, "she did begin by speaking

of her family in that rather strange way. So when I remembered, I thought I ought to tell you. Does it help? Does it fit with anything?"

Cecilia pursed her lips and nodded slowly.

"In an odd sort of way it may. The thing is, in Sister Barbara's file there's absolutely nothing about her family. *Nothing at all*, and I mean that literally. We're asking Joseph to look into it. At any rate, this is one more thing to put into the mix." She paused. "And it was something Rachel said that made you remember this?"

"We were talking about our picnic in Salmon Pool Lane, and how you were cold. And Rachel said, 'Mummy only came because she knew *we* all wanted to go.'"

"Did she! I'm sure *I* wasn't that perceptive when I was three years' old."

"I wasn't that perceptive last Saturday! Anyway, Rachel is very clear that next time we go on a picnic we have to pick a warm day, so that mummy doesn't get cold. I think, darling, you may have to face the fact that she loves you."

Cecilia laughed with pure joy.

"You know," she said, "I think perhaps she does!"

After Michael had rung off, Cecilia sat for several moments making notes to share with Verity and the others. Then her mobile rang again.

This time it was the pathologist. She hadn't expected anything so quickly, but suspicion of murder had presumably bumped Sister Barbara to the top of the queue.

"Quick preliminary report," he said. "Doctor Musgrave was quite right. It was strangulation—clear marks of thumbs and fingers on the throat. They were largish hands, so probably the killer was a man, and quite a big fellow. He was certainly taller than she was—which admittedly isn't saying much. She was a little bit of a thing. Quite certainly he was wearing leather gloves—and they left glove prints. If you can find those gloves for us, I dare say we can match them to the victim. Time of death is hard to estimate, as it was rather cold last night. Probably about midnight, but let's say between eleven and one-thirty a.m. to be on the safe side. That's all I can give you for now. I'll get a full autopsy report to you as soon as I can, and that may add something. But in any case you've definitely got a murder on your hands."

Cecilia talked briefly to her superior, Chief Superintendent Glyn Davies in Exeter, who asked her to convey his distress to the sisters, and confirmed her as senior investigating officer. There was sense in this, since she was on the spot and already knew something of the situation, but it was also a compliment, since normally Devon and Cornwall police placed a Detective Superintendent in charge of murder investigations.

She then took Verity with her to the orchard, and on the way told her what she had learned from her various phone conversations. They arrived to find the murder investigation team in full swing.

"Good morning, Tom," she said to Tom Foss, a medical doctor and one of the two scene-of-crime officers, "so have you anything for us yet?"

He shrugged.

"Obviously, the crime scene's compromised, but it's not all bad news. We've found evidence of a scuffle where the body must have laid. And just by there we found a set of footprints that don't belong to any of the sisters or anyone else we can identify. It's trainers. A man's, I'd imagine. Nike LeBron X, size 10s—so quite large. He, assuming it was a he, seems to have stood for some time under the trees over there." He pointed. "Walk behind me, will you?" They followed, treading where he indicated, to what was evidently a good vantage point. It had a view of the chapel door, and was itself fairly well secluded—anyone standing there at night would have been virtually invisible to the sisters.

"We've also found his entry point. Again, walk where I walk, will you?"

This time he led to them to a place in the abbey wall where scuffs in the soil suggested that someone had jumped down.

"As you see, the wall's quite low here. An able bodied person could get over easily enough. And there are several sets of footprints, all from the same Nike LeBron Xs. The point is, it looks as though he came over more than once. Three times, we reckon, judging by the marks. And it has to have been in the last three days, because on Saturday night you'll remember we had heavy rain, which would surely have washed the marks away."

"So he'd probably been watching the sisters—maybe even for a couple of days," Cecilia said.

He shrugged. "Looks like it. But here's the odd thing. There's *another* set of trainer prints, Karrimor Tempos, which look to coincide with the third set of our Mr. X's prints. In other words, the last time he came over, he seems to have brought a little friend."

"Little?"

"Well, no, not literally, though the prints are one size smaller, and I'd say the wearer was someone a bit lighter, although my guess would still be that it was a man. It looks to me as if they stood here together for a few minutes, and it looks as if Sister Barbara stood here with them for a bit, too. Maybe she joined them, or they found her here, or she found them. Anyway, then little friend—Mr. Y if you like—goes off on his own, over towards the main building. We'll check there later. The prints of Sister Barbara and Mr. X then suggest they took a little walk, over to where the scuffle marks are and her body was found. From there Mr. X's prints lead straight back to the wall. Mr. Y seems to come back more or less the way he came, and to climb back over the wall, *after* Mr. X — see how the Karrimor prints overlap the Nike's? Of course I can't tell how long after. It could be immediately after or it could be half an hour after."

"So let me make sure I've got this straight. On this last occasion Mr. X gets into the orchard over the wall as usual, but this time there's a Mr. Y with him. They meet or are met by Sister Barbara. They maybe have a chat. Then Mr. Y goes off towards the main building, while Mr. X and Sister Barbara take a little walk into the orchard, where Mr. X kills her. He then goes straight back from the orchard to the wall and over it. Mr. Y comes back from wherever he's been, doesn't go to where Sister Barbara's body is but goes straight to the wall and over it — *after* Mr. X but we don't know how long after. It could be immediately after or it could be a while. Is that it?"

"That's it — I think! Last but not least as far as the orchard is concerned, we found this on top of the wall."

He produced a plastic evidence bag with strands of dark blue thread in it. "It looks as if one of them snagged what he was wearing on the way over. Probably a tracksuit."

Cecilia nodded.

"Now come with me to the other side," he said.

In the road, Jack Gibbin, Foss's scene-of-crime-officer colleague, was working his way along the wall, peering at it. But the team had already marked part of it with blue and white "police-do-not-cross" tapes, and they soon saw why.

"There were two cars parked here last night," Foss said. "See the tire marks." He pointed to marks in the earth and grass by the road. "So far as I can see, the Nike trainers — our Mr. X — got out of this one, and the Karrimors — our Mr. Y — got out of this one. It looks," he pointed to marks in the grass, "as if both pairs of trainers stood there for several minutes. Then they went over the wall."

Cecilia nodded.

"I can't tell how long the cars were here, but judging by the tire marks, I do think the one with the Nike trainers, Mr. X, left first. It was parked behind the other, close up to it I think, and see how it seemed to have reversed a meter or so, so as to be able pull out and then round the car in front of it."

Again Cecilia nodded.

"There's one other thing." He produced a second plastic evidence bag, in which was the stub of a cigar. "This was in the ditch right by the marks from the trainers. Very clever of us to find it!"

She smiled.

"Most ingenious!"

"And you can see how it might have got there," he continued, theorizing with mounting enthusiasm. "They stand and look at the wall, one of them smoking, running through what they're planned to do. Then they decide it's time to go for it. The one that's smoking takes a last puff and throws his cigar away, so as to have his hands free to climb."

"Which would be pretty stupid," Verity said, "given everyone knows about DNA and all that these days."

He shrugged.

"People do stupid things. Especially when their minds are on something else — like what they're going to do next."

Cecilia frowned.

"But *what* were they going to do next? We know what Mr. X did. But what did Mr. Y get up to? At least it doesn't look as if anybody else got murdered."

"I'd have thought it most likely Mr. Y went to steal something," Verity said. "You said he went towards the main building?"

Cecilia nodded. "We'll have to have the sisters check to see if anything missing."

"And we'd better check for ourselves in and around the main building," Foss said. "There might be something."

Cecilia nodded — but then could not help herself.

"The cigar might, of course, be nothing to do with it. Someone could just have chucked it from a passing car."

Verity blew out her cheeks.

"Bit of a coincidence, though," she said, "for it to land just there."

Cecilia nodded.

"Of course you *will* check it for fingerprints? Saliva?"

"Of course. Unfortunately it fell in a puddle. But we can try back at the lab. Something may have survived. There is one other thing, though. Jack," —he nodded towards his colleague—"who claims to know about these things, says it's quite an expensive and special *sort* of cigar. He'll tell you what sort if you ask him nicely."

Jack Gibbin turned and approached.

"I don't think there's anything else along there," he said. "But do I hear someone calling my name? As long as it's not the owl yet, I don't mind."

"Tell us about the cigar," Verity said.

"Oh, yes, the cigar! It's a Flor De Oliva Robusto, and a box of twenty-five of them will set you back about a hundred and fifty quid, or possibly more, depending where you buy them. In other words—this is not exactly your average quick drag."

"Well," Verity said, "it's certainly satisfying to know one is looking for a murderer who has good taste. It lends such an air of *elegance* to our investigations!"

Ten

Cecilia divided up the individual interviews between them.
"I perceive," Verity said, peering at the sheet Cecilia
had given her, "that *you* have the intelligent and interesting
Mother Evelyn to talk to, and also the beautiful and observant
Sister Chiara, whereas *I* and PC Jarman are landed with the
obnoxious Father Carlton."

"That's true," Cecilia said. "Rank hath its privileges."

She relented.

"Actually," she said, "I think I've already met Father Carlton
at a diocesan affair with my other hat on as Michael's wife, and
I don't want roles to get muddled."

Verity nodded. "Got it."

"Anyway," Cecilia added, "I'd like you with me when I talk
with Sister Chiara. And I've also provided you and PC Jarman
with naughty Sister Agnes, who will surely be fun, and Dick
Posan, the man what can and does, who sounds like just the
sort of chap one wants to be around."

"Consider me mollified," Verity said.

***

Cecilia intended to call Mother Evelyn and arrange to see her. But before she could do that, Mother Evelyn called her.

"Chief Inspector, I've made a disturbing discovery. Do you mind coming to the office?"

"I'm on my way."

She took PC Wilkins with her. They found Mother Evelyn sitting at a large, old-fashioned desk with several ledgers and account books and a laptop computer in front of her. Dismas, who was sitting by the desk in a battered dog bed, gave a conversational woof and thumped his tail at their entry.

"Mother, you said you'd made a disturbing discovery."

"Oh yes, I'm afraid I have—*very* disturbing. And I think it might have some connection with poor Barbara's death."

She rose to her feet.

"I was intending to check the books this morning. As we told you, Sister Barbara was our treasurer and to tell you the truth I don't really know who can replace her. But then after I got the ledgers out I decided to spend a few moments in our meditation room. Come and see what I found when I went in."

Cecilia and PC Wilkins followed her along a passage.

"It's helpful to have a small space for prayer in the main building," Mother Evelyn said. "Sometimes one needs a moment or so of recollection, and it isn't always convenient to go across to the chapel. So the bishop consecrated this for us."

"Actually, the problem isn't what I found here, but what I didn't find," she said as they reached the door. She opened it onto peaceful, windowless room furnished with cushions and a couple of prie-dieux. In the wall to their right was an aumbry, with a light. Otherwise the walls were bare.

"What *should* be facing us," she said, "is an oil painting of Our Lady and the Infant Christ. It's eighteenth century, and it's been in our community's possession since we received it as gift from Bishop Henry Philpotts when he founded us in 1853. It's very precious to us."

Cecilia had a sharp intake of breath.

"You all sleep at the other end of the building, Mother. Is that right?"

"Yes, and I'm afraid the door wasn't even latched. So someone could easily have come in and we'd probably not hear. Actually—"

She stopped.

"Yes, Mother?"

Mother Evelyn sighed. "Actually, Dismas was grumbling quite a lot last night, which isn't like him. He even barked, once. He usually sleeps like a log. Perhaps I should have listened to him."

And perhaps, Cecilia reflected, it was just as well you didn't, or we might have had two murders on our hands. But she said nothing.

"Do you have any idea what the painting was worth?" she asked.

"Five hundred thousand pounds."

"That's very precise."

"As it happens we'd just had it valued. Here's the valuation. I got it out of the file while I was waiting for you just now."

She passed a sheet to Cecilia, who looked at it, and showed it to Wilkins.

The evaluation had been conducted by a firm called Clark and Gregson, with addresses in London and Exeter.

Clark and Gregson described the painting as an oil sketch, noting that it was the work of the late eighteenth century Italian painter Gian Domenico Tiepolo. The sisters were strenuously advised not even to consider selling it for anything less than five hundred thousand pounds and to insure it for at that sum.

"So was the community thinking of selling it?"

"We'd thought about it very seriously. Sister Barbara told me that she had even talked to an art dealer who made us a generous offer. And the money would really have helped with our apostolate."

"Which is?"

"We visit the lonely and we try to relieve the poor. That's what Bishop Phillpotts founded us to do. There was a lot of loneliness and poverty in north Devon in those days, and even now in the welfare state — or such relics of it as the wretched politicians have left us — there's still more of both than people might think. Sometimes helping the poor is just a matter of helping them get what they're entitled to — helping them fill in forms and things. But sometimes we need to do something for them ourselves. So it would be nice to have a bit more, indeed, a substantial bit more, in our funds."

Cecilia nodded.

But Mother Evelyn had obviously not finished singing the praises of her sisters.

"Of course some of us do other things," she said. "It would be sinful to waste people's talents. Sister Chiara is brilliant, so of course we encourage her to study and write. She's already had two papers published in *Sobornost*! I know the bishop hopes she'll discern a vocation to the priesthood in time. Then we could have the Eucharist every day!" She sighed. "I did ask Sister Barbara once if she'd thought about the priesthood. She certainly had gifts for it. But she was adamant she couldn't even consider it."

"That's very strong. Did she say why?"

"No. Just stated it as a fact. And she was someone who — well, one did not argue with her on such a matter. One felt that she knew who she was."

Cecilia nodded. There was a pause. She looked again towards the blank wall of the meditation room.

"Do you know who the art dealer was?"

"I'm afraid I don't. But I'm sure there'll be a note about it in Sister Barbara's diary. She was very methodical."

"Perhaps the man who came to see her the other day was from the art dealer? The man Sister Chiara described? The man nobody knew?"

"Perhaps he was."

"Anyway, the community decided not to sell the picture?"

"We were wavering. But then we received a small legacy — twenty thousand pounds — and we thought perhaps that was a sign we should at least wait a little, and see what God brought us, before we parted with the painting of Our Lady and her Child. It *is* a part of our history, as well as being beloved by us. And Bishop Phillpotts clearly intended that it should be prayed over, as it is here — indeed, that's surely what the artist intended. Not for it to sit in a museum or somebody's art collection."

Cecilia nodded.

"The painting is insured, I take it?"

"Yes."

Again Cecilia nodded, and looked again around the meditation room.

"I'm afraid, Mother, that all this means we're going to have to treat this as a crime scene too — check for prints, and so on. Sister Barbara would have worked at that desk in the main office? Those were the ledgers and books and the computer she used?"

"Yes."

"Someone will come and look at those, too. That will probably be this afternoon. It will be Joseph Stirrup, our computer specialist. He'll try to disturb you as little as possible, but he may need to take things away."

"I understand, Chief Inspector."

"PC Wilkins, will you go and brief the scene-of-crime officers about this?"

"Yes, ma'am."

Cecilia turned back to Mother Evelyn.

"One last question. Who do you think knew that the painting was here? And knew what it was?"

"Well our community, obviously. We've always known. And Clark and Gregson—the firm that did our evaluation. And I suppose whoever the art dealer was who made the offer. That's probably all. I mean, we don't go about saying, 'We've got a valuable painting in our meditation room.' We don't think of it like that."

Cecilia nodded. And that, she reflected, made all of them who *did* know into suspects. Technically, even the sisters. Even Mother Evelyn. They could have organized the theft themselves. And theoretically, one or all of them could have had a motive for organizing Sister Barbara's death.

She pursed her lips, and sighed. One of the sadder aspects of her work was that again and again it obliged her to consider the worst possibilities in the nicest people. The only good news in all this was that she now surely had a possible motive for someone to kill Sister Barbara.

A half of a million pounds' worth of it.

ELEVEN

St. Boniface Abbey, a few minutes later.

Mother Evelyn, Cecilia, and PC Wilkins returned to the main office.

"You and Sister Barbara knew each other for a long time, I imagine?" Cecilia said.

"Ever since I came back in 1994."

"Came back?"

"Back to Devon. I grew up in South Moulton."

"But you left for while?"

"I was drawn to the big city, I suppose! I joined the Community of Saint John the Divine in Birmingham in 1985, and I was with them until '94. But then my mother, who was still in South Moulton, became very fragile. Dad had died some years before. So the Bishops of Birmingham and Exeter agreed I should join the sisters here so as to be near her. She died in 1998 and I suppose I could have gone back to Birmingham. But by then God seemed to have found a place for me here, so here I stayed."

"And Sister Barbara was here when you arrived?"

"She'd been here since 1993. She'd just been accepted as a novice when I arrived, and made her full profession in 1999."

"Would you say it's a happy place, Mother?"

"We have our ups and downs like everyone else. But overall yes, I'd say we're happy. For me it's been the happiest place in the world. Until this."

Cecilia nodded.

"And can you think of anything in Sister Barbara's behavior over recent weeks that seemed at all odd or unusual to you? Anything that might have suggested she was troubled, or anxious? However trivial it seemed at the time, it might be relevant."

Mother Evelyn considered.

"There's one thing," she said, "though it may not be relevant."

Cecilia made her "encouraging" noise, and waited.

"About eight weeks ago—I can get you the exact date if you want—she asked permission to go to London for the day. She said there was someone she'd been very close to before her profession—someone whose life had been anything but what it should be—and he'd just died. She wanted to visit his grave and pray for his repose. Of course one might argue she could have prayed for him just as well here, and so she could. But Christianity has never scorned the physical—ours is, after all, the religion of the incarnation—and if she sensed a call to go to where the body had been laid, I wouldn't dismiss it. So I gave permission. Would you like the exact date?"

Cecilia glanced at Wilkins.

"I think we would."

Mother Evelyn went to her desk, brought out a diary from the drawer, and turned pages.

"Here we are. It was Wednesday, the eleventh of September. Almost exactly eight weeks ago."

"I don't suppose she said who this person was, or anything about their relationship?"

"No, and while of course I'd have listened if she'd volunteered anything, you'll understand that I wouldn't have considered it proper to ask. I trust the sisters."

Cecilia nodded.

"So—did she drive to London? Take the train?"

"Sister Chiara drove her to Exeter and saw her onto the train to Paddington."

"Do you know which train?"

"I think it was about ten o'clock. Chiara will probably know exactly."

Again Cecilia nodded. It sounded like the 9:58.

"And would she have been wearing her habit?"

"Oh, yes."

So she will have been quite a distinctive figure.

"The photograph of Sister Barbara in her habit that's in the file—do you know it?"

"I put it there."

"It's a good likeness?"

"I think so."

"Thank you. And did Sister Chiara bring her back to the abbey, after her visit to London?"

"Yes. Barbara came home on an afternoon train and Chiara collected her at the station. By the time they got back to the abbey they'd missed Evensong and the news—on weekdays we always watch the BBC news so as to stay in touch—and they had to have their supper late. But they were in time for Compline. I remember that."

"And how did Sister Barbara seem after all this?"

"At peace. Which was enough for me. Neither of us referred to the matter again."

TWELVE

Verity joined Cecilia as she was walking towards the chapel, and was told what had happened in the interview with Mother Evelyn.

At mention of the missing painting, and even more when she heard its value, Verity's eyes gleamed.

"Now *that's* what I call a motive! And now it's pretty clear what our Mr. Y was up to."

"Evidently! What's *not* clear is how our two crimes relate to each other. Was the art theft the real point and the murder collateral damage? — Sister Barbara just happening to be in the wrong place at the wrong moment? Or was Sister Barbara the intended *target*, and the theft opportunistic? Or did someone really plan to do *both*? And how — if at all — does any or all of it link to Sister Barbara going to London in September? I wouldn't half like to know whose grave she visited!"

"Assuming," Verity said, "she visited a grave at all."

"Do you have reason to think she didn't?"

"No. But I do have this friend who is also my superior officer who regularly says, 'what we can't show, we don't know.'"

Cecilia laughed.

"Point taken! Anyway, let's send the photograph of Sister

Barbara to the Met, and maybe someone can show it around Paddington Station. It's a long shot, but Mother Evelyn says she was wearing her habit, so it's just possible someone may recall seeing a nun getting off a train from the West Country eight weeks ago. If it was the 9:58 — I dare say the observant Sister Chiara will confirm that — she should have arrived at Paddington at about half past twelve. Of course we can check that, too."

"I'm on it. And now would you like to hear how Constable Jarman and I got on with Father Carlton?"

"Absolutely!"

"He answered the door wearing one of those cassocks with buttons all the way down the front and a flappy cape thing that I believe is known in the trade as a *pellegrina*. We'd barely identified ourselves before he was giving us a detailed recital of his diary for the next two days, from which we were to understand that he was terribly busy, pressured by constant demands and crushing burdens of responsibility, and really didn't have time to waste on little matters like talking to me and PC Jarman. He addressed all this, incidentally, directly to PC Jarman, as if I wasn't really there."

Cecilia nodded. That was rather how she remembered him. It had, of course, been a social event, not a police investigation. But he'd been one of those people who keep looking past you while you're having a conversation with them, so that you end up feeling that you are something of an interruption, stopping them from getting to the person they really want to talk to.

"So then?"

"PC Jarman, to his undying credit, just let the man rattle on until at last he ran out of steam. When that finally happened I then explained to the good father that we too were terribly busy. All day. But that this was a murder inquiry, and the police took murder rather seriously — and I rather thought the church did too. So it might be a good idea if he were to answer our questions."

Cecilia smiled. She would bet on Verity Jones being able to handle a pompous priest any day.

"And so?"

"He doesn't like the sisters. Thinks they're an anachronism. Which is ironic, since if you ask me he's a bit of an anachronism himself. Anyway, he's particularly annoyed with Mother Evelyn. Apparently a couple of days back she was delivering some charitable donations the sisters had collected to the rectory while he was trying to chat up some terribly rich London chap called Kellog who's just moved into Blomfield and might give the town some money towards a new clinic."

Blomfield was a small, very exclusive and very expensive group of new houses to the west of the town.

"So?"

"So evidently either the brakes on the nuns' car or Mother Evelyn's driving aren't as good as they might be, and when she parked outside the rectory she ran into the back of Mr. Kellog's Rolls Royce. They heard the bang from Father Carlton's study, and Mr. Kellog went out to see what had happened. When he got there, apparently Mother Evelyn told him he shouldn't have been parked there and his enormous car was blocking up the road and being a nuisance. She said it quite loudly — Father Carlton could hear it from his study. So then Mr. Kellog got annoyed and had something of an altercation with her. Then he drove off — without giving his donation to the clinic. So Father Carlton had wasted his valuable morning. I suppose to be fair to Father Carlton he does have a point. I mean, so far as I can see she did drive into the back of the fellow's perfectly legally parked car."

Cecilia nodded.

"Well, as an upshot of all this I was beginning to think that if anyone had a motive for murdering a nun it was Father Carlton.

Maybe he even *thought* he'd murdered Mother Evelyn and got the wrong one. I dare say one small, middle-aged, bespectacled nun looks much the same as another in the dark. But before I could work out the details of this fiendishly clever theory, I thought I'd better ask him where he was last night between 11:00 and 1:30. To my great regret it turns out that he's got an alibi. He was with college friends celebrating Guy Fawkes in Clovelly, stayed the whole night, and he'd only just got back to Edgestow when I turned up. I got the names and we'll want to check them of course, but I don't think there's much future there. Though I hate to admit it, I rather think he's telling the truth."

"Get his alibi checked, certainly," Cecilia said. "And, I suppose, Mr. Kellog too. We need to know everything. This is going to involve a lot of legwork. Jarman and Wilkins can get going on that."

She looked at her watch.

"We, on the other hand, can get going with lunch."

THIRTEEN

The Great Western public house, a little before noon.

They were early at The Great Western, which was what Cecilia had intended, and the bar was still empty. Jim Pettigrew the landlord was an innkeeper in the best tradition, which meant that although his pub always gave an impression of being spotless — gleaming glass and shining brass and immaculate polished wood — it was also welcoming to all: business suits and dresses from the bank and the local law office, muddy wellingtons and dogs from the farms, children and harassed mums from anywhere. All of which meant that from noon onwards it would be packed.

Jim Pettigrew bustled forward with a welcoming smile as they entered.

"Chief Inspector! Sergeant! And Mr. Stirrup! Good to see you all! Will it be the usual?"

"Not today, Jim! We're on duty. But we'd all like some of your fish and chips, please."

She nodded towards the menu board, which announced proudly, "Our fish arrives fresh caught from Ilfracombe every morning. Our vegetables are local and organic."

"And I'll have San Pellegrino to drink," she added.

Verity ordered the same. So did Joseph Stirrup, who had joined them for lunch.

"We'll sit in our usual booth, Jim," Cecilia said, "and I wonder if you could spare Jennifer to sit and talk with us for a few minutes, at least until you start to get busy? I'd like to hear from her about her impressions of the abbey. I gather she goes there quite often."

"Yes, of course," Jim said. "What a terrible business! Who on earth would want to do such a thing to such nice ladies beats me."

"To tell you the truth, Jim, just at the moment it beats us. Which is why we're talking to everybody, trying to get a picture."

Jennifer Pettigrew brought them their San Pellegrino after a few minutes. She was a tall, well-built, pleasant looking girl with long dark hair tied back in a ponytail.

"Monica is cooking your fish now. She'll be along with your lunches as soon she's got them ready," she said. "But Dad said you wanted to talk to me."

Cecilia nodded. "Jennifer, tell me about your visits to the abbey."

"Well, I go up there twice a week, once to collect the produce, and once to take the money for it. We generally use most of it ourselves — it's always beautiful, and of course it's organic. But anything we can't use, there's a market holder I take it to, and he's happy to buy it. It might be any of the sisters who I get the produce from, but it's always Sister Barbara I see when we settle up." She hesitated, then said, "It's ... it's her, isn't it?"

Quite how news circulates in a small town, Cecilia had never understood. But it did, and she had some time ago given up trying to keep account or track of it. She nodded. "I'm afraid so."

Jennifer shook her head. "That's horrible. She was a good lady, and very kind."

"Do you say that for any special reason?" Cecilia said.

"Well yes. I was having real boyfriend trouble a few months back, and she saw something was wrong and asked me about it and I found myself telling her. And you know because they're nuns people think they're going to start going on at you about God, but she really listened to me. And then she pointed out to me some of the things I was saying—I mean, it was like she understood what I was saying better than I did! And it really helped. She was a good lady."

'Twas a good lady. 'Twas a good lady. We may pick o'er a thousand salads ere we light on such another herb.

Papa would always say that line when she was little and they read Shakespeare's *All's Well That Ends Well* together. And always when he did, it made her want to cry, though she never knew why. And now Jennifer had tears in her eyes. So perhaps this was why? Do plays give you words for things that haven't happened to you yet?

There was a pause.

"And you last visited the sisters …?"

"Yesterday morning ma'am. To take the money."

"So you saw Sister Barbara?"

"Yes, ma'am. Just like always."

"Did she seem different in any way from usual?"

"No, ma'am, I don't think so. She made her little joke about me being the lady with the moneybags, just like she always does … did …"

She stopped.

A couple of farmers came in with their dogs, followed by a group of young men and women from an office. Suddenly the bar was starting to fill up.

"I think, ma'am, I ought to go if you don't mind. Dad will be needing me."

"That's fine for now. And thank you, Jennifer. You've been very helpful. We might ask you some more questions later if we think of any. And if you think of anything else, you know how to find me."

"I do. Thank you ma'am. And ... and ... I hope you catch whoever did it ma'am."

"So do I, Jennifer! So do I! By the way, it seems an odd thing to say in a pub—but there's a terrible smell of stale beer round here. I didn't notice it when I came in—it's not at the bar. It's just round here."

"Yes there is." Jennifer had risen to her feet. She bent towards a plant that was on the sill beside their table. "Here it is! Someone's been pouring his drink into it last night I dare say. I should have caught it when I cleaned up."

"Why on earth would anyone pour his drink into a plant?" Joseph asked.

Jennifer shook her head.

"It's daft, I'll grant you. But young men do it all the time when they think nobody's looking, wanting to impress their girlfriends with how much they can drink."

"And the poor things think we don't notice!" Verity added.

The two young women laughed.

"Oh Lord," Cecilia thought to herself, suddenly remembering her late ex-husband, "that's exactly what George used to do!"

"I'll take it away and give it a proper drink," Jennifer said. "It'll soon feel better."

She gathered pot and plant in strong arms, and departed.

Cecilia and Verity had just about brought Joseph up to date with the morning's developments and the fact that they now had two crimes on their hands and no clear idea how they related to each other, when Monica brought their fish and chips and peas.

"Those look wonderful," Joseph said.

"That cod was swimming happily in the sea twenty-four hours ago, and the beer batter and the chips is all fresh made.

Proper chips, as you see—not them nasty little French-fry things!"

Joseph nodded.

"Truly *British* chips," he said loyally.

"Isn't it traditional to serve mushy peas with fish and chips?" Verity asked—"Not that these peas aren't delicious," she added hastily. "I was just curious."

"You'll find that's the way they do it a lot in the north," Monica said. "Places like Yorkshire and Lancashire. And if all you've got is dried peas, it's as good as anything. I do it sometimes in winter. But these are beautiful fresh Balmorals—I think they'll be the last of the season, we don't usually have them after October, but it's been a wonderful growing summer—and I think it'd be a sin to do anything but cook them very lightly."

"They're lovely!" Cecilia said.

Monica left them and there followed a lengthy pause during which they sampled her cooking and made suitably appreciative remarks. Then,

"Verity," Cecilia said, "when there's a good moment, I want someone to get together with Jim Pettigrew and Jennifer, and see how many people they remember seeing here last night between 11:00 and 1:30. And since he had an altercation with at least *a* sister, I'd like to know where Mr. Kellog says he was between those times. You can get uniform to help with some of that. It's fairly routine stuff. You could let Wilkins and Jarman have a go at some of it together, rather than each just trailing round after us."

"I'll do it, ma'am."

"And you said you'd be checking on Father Carlton's alibi—those people he says he was with in Clovelly?"

"I called while I was waiting for you just now. Local uniform have promised to do it this afternoon."

"Good. Now, Joseph, I know you're already working on Sister Barbara's life before she became a nun."

"I made a start this morning but I haven't really got anywhere yet."

"Well, I still want to know about her. But there are some other things, too. I'd like you to go to the abbey this afternoon, and go through the books and ledgers Sister Barbara used, and also check that computer of hers. I've told Mother Evelyn to expect you. See if you notice anything useful. I particularly want to know who the art dealer was who offered to buy the painting. And I'd like you to check on the people who did the evaluation for the sisters—it's a firm called Clark and Gregson."

Joseph nodded.

"All right," he said. "I dare say I can cope with that."

"And I always thought art theft was a rather genteel sort of crime!" Verity said.

"Not any more it isn't," Cecilia said. "The thieves who stole paintings from the Munch Museum a few years back were masked and waving guns and had an escape car outside."

"That's right," Joseph said. "Oslo. August 2004. Clean as a whistle, but hardly genteel!"

Fourteen

Edgestow. A few minutes later.

Cecilia and Verity parted from Joseph in The Great Western car park, and returned to the Abbey. It was time, Cecilia decided, for their interview with Sister Chiara.

Just inside the front door to the main building they found Sister Agnes.

"I think Chiara will be in the chapel," Sister Agnes said. "She's taken over as sacristan for this week, and the bishop's coming tomorrow."

They went back to the chapel—which was a basically a tiny medieval church with a few Tudor modifications—and entered by the west door. The light within was golden, almost Mediterranean: an effect, evidently, of the glass. Cecilia found it quite breathtaking, and paused to take it in. Verity stopped slightly behind her.

They walked slowly forward through the nave, mounted the sanctuary steps, and came to the altar rail. As they stood there, Eliot's words came to her.

You are not here to verify
Instruct yourself, or inform curiosity
Or carry report. You are here to kneel
Where prayer has been valid.

Almost involuntarily, she knelt. She sensed rather than heard Verity kneel beside her.

How long she was there she wasn't sure, but a noise behind her brought her abruptly back to the present. She looked round.

It was Sister Chiara, carrying a pile of books.

They spoke simultaneously.

"I'm so sorry, I disturbed you!"

"I'm sorry, we're in your way!"

"How could you possibly be in the way?" Chiara said as Cecilia and Verity got to their feet. She put down the books. "The bishop's coming tomorrow to spend some time with us and celebrate a requiem for Barbara, and Mother Evelyn thinks there'll be quite a lot of people. So there was a bit to get ready." She waved at the books. "But it's about done now. Agnes said you wanted to talk to me."

"We do. Is now a good time?"

"Of course."

Chiara sat down on a stall, and indicated that Cecilia and Verity should sit beside her.

"As a start," Cecilia said, "please, tell us something about the order, and how you come to be here. You seem rather younger than the others."

Chiara laughed. "You mean, what's a nice girl like me doing in a joint like this?"

Cecilia smiled. "Something like that!"

"Actually, I may not be the only one of my age here after next year. There are two others — friends of mine from Oxford — who are coming to try out their vocations in January. So who knows what may happen?"

Cecilia nodded.

"But how do *you* come to be here?"

"Well," Sister Chiara said, "it's all remarkably unremarkable. No Damascus road visions or dramas to report! Mummy and Daddy are lawyers and we were always quite well off and I had a lovely childhood. I was a very ordinary girl and liked all the ordinary things like boys and clothes and having a good time."

Cecilia gave what she hoped was an encouraging nod.

"We were Church of England," Chiara continued, "but not specially religious. We'd go to church for Christmas and Easter and Remembrance Sunday, and that was about it. The first thing about me that I suppose you might say was a bit odd was I got turned on to poetry. We had a wonderful English teacher at school. 'Shakespeare matters,' she'd say to us. 'You want to know *why*? Listen to the great soliloquies! You don't get it? Listen again! Keep on listening until you *do* get it!' 'How do I know it will be worth the effort?' I said to her one day. 'You can't know!' she said. 'Not until you've done it. That's half the fun.' So I decided I *would* make the effort and I went up to Girton to read English."

"Girton?"

"Cambridge," Verity said.

"Yes — I was lucky enough to get a scholarship. And that was where I made my great discovery — not mine in the sense that I invented it, but mine in that I realized it for myself."

"And that was?"

"Well, it seemed — *seems* — to me that poets — and I'd say musicians too, and artists generally — they're always saying, *look deeper* at the world! Look at precisely what people like poor Stephen Hawking don't seem able to grasp! Look at what's *beyond* what you can analyze or calculate, beyond the atoms and the particles! Then you'll see there's something *else* going on. Something important."

"*More than cool reason ever comprehends?*" Cecilia said.

That had always been Papa's line when they read *Midsummer Night's Dream*. He'd be Theseus and she'd be Hippolyta. She'd always rather fancied herself as Queen of the Amazons.

"Exactly!" Chiara said. "Even when they're personally unbelievers, the poet in them says that. Of course I realize that some scientists do it too. But it was the poets who did it for me, at least at first. Do you know Hardy's poem, *The Darkling Thrush*?"

Cecilia and Verity both shook their heads.

"Hardy is out in this terrible winter evening on the last night of the nineteenth century. Everything is cold and dead and totally depressing. Then suddenly this tiny, beaten up old thrush starts to sing—and blows Hardy's mind.

> *So little cause for carolings*
> *Of such ecstatic sound*
> *Was written on terrestrial things*
> *Afar or nigh around,*
> *That I could think there trembled through*
> *His happy good-night air*
> *Some blessed Hope, whereof he knew*
> *And I was unaware."*

Chiara had a beautiful voice and total commitment to the lines, and Cecilia caught her breath.

"Well," Chiara said, "listening to the poets, I *did* find myself looking deeper, and I believe I found God—or more precisely, God found me."

Cecilia nodded.

"And yet," she said, "not everyone who finds God ends up, as you put it, in a joint like this!"

Chiara laughed.

"In the Easter term of my second year Sister Agnes came to Oxford to help with a mission to the university. We became friends almost at once. We always seem able to make each other laugh. She's so funny and sensible she totally blew my mind about what nuns were like! So then I came and stayed here a few times. I watched the life they led and after a while I began to think maybe that was the life I wanted too."

She paused.

"We don't do it lightly, you know. After I'd said I was

interested in trying my vocation I lived here for a whole year as a postulant. Then I was a novice for two years, and then took Junior Vows for three more years. I only made my Life Profession last Easter. That's what will happen with Julie and Rose if they decide to come. We won't let them rush into it."

Julie and Rose were, presumably, the two friends from Oxford.

"How well did you know Sister Barbara?" Verity asked.

"She was important to me. Mother Evelyn appointed her to be my soul friend at the beginning of my novitiate." She hesitated. "I have my demons, like all of us. Sister Barbara seemed to understand them. She had a way of listening that made you feel you were the only person in the world for her at that moment, and then when she spoke, you felt she really understood why you were troubled. She'd been there."

"How do you mean — she'd been there?" Cecilia asked.

"She knew what it was like to feel vulnerable, out on a limb — not doing the things everyone thinks you ought to be doing."

Cecilia nodded.

"Forgive me asking this — it's rather delicate and I wouldn't normally dream of it, but this is a murder inquiry — would you have any idea just what Sister Barbara's demons might have been?"

Chiara pursed her lips, sighed, and slowly shook her head.

"No, not really. Of course it was my stuff we talked about — that's what we were there for."

She hesitated for a moment.

"Actually," she said, "there was one time that might have something to do with what you're asking. I said something about wondering what my parents would think if I joined the order. Barbara's mouth tightened. Then she said, 'Families are important, but you can't always do what they want. Sometimes they ask awful things of you.' I think that was the only time in our conversations when I felt, just for a moment, that she wasn't really with me. She was thinking about something else. Or some*one* else."

Cecilia drew in her breath sharply.

That was almost exactly what Michael had heard Sister Barbara say. And yet there was *nothing* about her family in the file that Mother Evelyn had given them.

She exchanged a glance with Verity, who gave a faint, almost imperceptible nod, and took up the questioning.

"A few weeks ago you took Sister Barbara up to Exeter, to the station, to go to London. Did she say anything about why she needed to go? While you were driving to Exeter, perhaps?"

Chiara shook her head.

"In the morning she was quiet and thoughtful. I didn't intrude on her. But when I picked her up in the evening, she was glowing. I must have asked the kind of vague question one does ask—'How has your day gone?' or 'Did you have a successful visit?' or something, and I remember her words better than my own. I think I have them more or less exactly. She said, 'It was wonderful! I knelt at the grave of a man I once knew and I prayed for his peace. And I felt he accepted that peace. And then, as if to validate my feeling, something happened that I couldn't have expected in my wildest dreams. I saw two people standing looking at me who I'd thought were lost to me forever. And I found they still loved me. We hugged and promised to pray for each other always, even though we may never see each other in this life again. So I am happy.' That's the gist of what she said."

"That's an amazing story," Verity said.

Chiara nodded.

"But that was it," she said. "We spent the rest of the drive back talking about what I'd been reading: Lewis's *Discarded Image*. She was something of a fan of *The Discarded Image*."

"And she gave you no clue who the person she prayed for

might have been? Beyond calling him 'him'? Or who the long-lost people she saw might have been?"

"No. And I didn't feel it right to ask. But—in view of what she said in that other conversation—perhaps they were members of her family."

There was a pause.

"So *was* your family upset with your choice of career?" Verity asked.

Chiara laughed.

"I was worrying for nothing. Mummy says she wants me to be happy and if this is what I want it's fine by her. Daddy says he always thought I'd end up doing something like this, though I can't imagine why he'd have thought that."

Perhaps, Cecilia reflected, it was because you were never quite such an ordinary girl as you think.

Fifteen

Edgestow, early that afternoon.

In the latter part of the afternoon Verity took PC Jarman with her to call on Dick Posan, who was at home with his wife Patti. They received cups of tea from Patti, together with small and delicious cakes that she had made following recipes handed down from Dick's father, who had been Serbian and had worked on the railways and also been a wonderful baker.

In addition to these indulgences, they also learned that the sisters of Saint Boniface were in general highly regarded in the community, chiefly because they visited the elderly and lonely. Neither Dick nor Patti could think of the slightest reason why anyone would want to hurt Sister Barbara, or, indeed, any of them, and they were both totally horrified at what had happened. At the time of the murder, they had been with other celebrators of Guy Fawkes in The Great Western.

Verity and Jarman then returned to the convent and interviewed Sister Agnes—which turned out to be just as amusing and interesting as Cecilia thought it might be. In her former life Sister Agnes had been an actress, and three times married—"after which, my dears, I'd had quite enough of men—no offence intended, constable, I'm sure you're quite charming and some lovely young woman will be delighted to have you—but I'd had enough of men and I admired what the sisters were doing so I decided I wanted to join the order. Fortunately for me they were very gracious and decided they'd have me, warts and all."

"Were your divorces amicable, Sister?" PC Jarman asked.

Agnes laughed.

"If you mean, darling, are my ex-husbands so angry with me for abandoning them that one of them might have decided to come here and murder one of us just to make a point— then no, I think I may fairly confidently say that won't have happened. My divorces were amicable in the sense that by the time they happened my husbands were just as bored with me as I was with them, so we were all quite happy to part company."

"Sometimes people quarrel about property," Verity said.

Agnes laughed again.

"We were all of us reasonably successful actors," she said, "but not *very* successful. We were the kind you see in an episode of something on television and think to yourself, 'I can't remember her name, but I'm sure I saw her in something else last month. What was it?' Only then you can't remember the name of that either! By all of which I mean we made a decent living but not a fortune. And by *that* I mean, we wouldn't have quarreled about property because none of us ever had enough property to be worth quarreling about!"

Somehow—Verity admitted that in all honesty that she wasn't quite sure how, and PC Jarman's notes didn't seem to answer the question either—the interview got round to the subject of Father Carlton.

"Well, yes, he *is* a pompous ass! And he reads the liturgy as if it were the telephone directory—but then, that's true of a lot of priests. Physically they're standing right there in front of you, but the fact is they aren't really *present* at all. They don't understand performance."

"Surely, sister, a priest oughtn't to be *performing*?" Verity said. "That sounds to me like faking it!"

"You are confusing performance with bad acting, my dear. Performance — true performance, which includes *good* acting — is when words are taken off a page, where they were just marks on paper, and *formed again through a person* — restored to their proper element — which is sound, and breath, and life. And it's not just a matter of *saying* them. It's a matter of *intending* them — as, of course, we naturally intend our words when we speak to each other, especially when we're saying things that matter to us. For real performance, it's not enough to know what words mean, you have to *experience* them, *in that moment*. Your heart has to be in it. Good actors do that. And some priests do it when they celebrate the liturgy. And however quiet and low key they may be, you can always tell. Father Carlton doesn't. Your Chief Inspector's Father Michael does."

"He came and conducted a retreat for you earlier in the year, I think?"

"That's right. The first three days of Holy Week. And when he said mass it was wonderful. Now if *he* could be our chaplain … but then of course we realize he's at the other end of the diocese and he's got a parish to run."

"So you knew that DCI Cavaliere was married to a priest? — to Father Michael?"

"Oh yes, my dear," Agnes said. "Everyone in Edgestow knows it! And of course we understand she has to keep her role clear as a police officer, so we haven't brought it up. But at least it's nice to know we're being investigated by someone who isn't going to assume that just because we're religious we must all be batty!"

Perhaps the sisters had been watching *Midsomer Murders*, too?

"Given what you say about a good actor's attitude to words," Verity said, "about taking them and intending them *in the moment*, it seems to me that if they wanted to be, actors would be extremely good liars."

"Oh yes, my dear, they certainly would! Including me. I'm a wonderful liar!"

At 5:00 p.m. Cecilia and Verity met in the incident room with PCs Wilkins and Jarman.

PCs Wilkins and Jarman were able to report on interviews that they had conducted together with Sisters Athanasius and Francis, neither of whom had been able to add anything of significance to what the police already knew. The two constables had then driven out to Blomfield and visited the wealthy Mr. Kellog. He claimed to have been in The Great Western from 10:00 p.m. on the night of the murder. His wife and friends of theirs had joined him at about 11:00, and they'd been together there until it closed at 1:30. Then he'd gone home with Mrs. Kellog. Mrs. Kellog agreed with this story. Finally the officers had gone back to The Great Western and got from the Pettigrews a list of people the landlord and his daughter could remember seeing in the pub between 11:00 and 1:30. The list included Mr. and Mrs. Kellog and their friends as well as Dick and Patti Posan, to that extent confirming all their stories.

As they were completing their report, Cecilia's mobile rang.

"DCI Cavaliere," she said.

"It's Joseph. You wanted to know about the firm that did the sisters' evaluation for them—Clark and Gregson."

"Yes."

"Established 1876. They do a lot of evaluations for the Church of England. No doubt that's why the sisters used them. London based, but there's a branch in Exeter. All very respectable. 'Nothing known against them' is, I believe, the proper phrase."

"All right."

"Now would you like the good news?"

"There is some?"

"I've found out who offered to buy the painting. It's Abrahams Fine Art of Exeter on West Street. Family firm. They've been there since 1946. It's open Monday to Friday, nine 'til five. There's a letter from them here, signed by Saul Abrahams, who is, I take it, the boss. He offers £525,000 for it — quite a lot over the estimate, you'll note."

"Sounds as if he was anxious to get it."

Anxious enough to kill one of the sisters?

Her conversation with Joseph over, Cecilia put the 'phone back into her bag and told the others.

"Clearly we need to talk to Mr. Abrahams and Messrs. Clark and Gregson. What is it Sherlock Holmes says at moments like this?"

"The game is afoot," Verity said. "Though I must say I've never thought him half as clever as some people seem to. That thing of his about 'eliminating the impossible' is silly."

"It is?"

"It assumes you know what's possible. And of course no one does."

Sixteen

West Street, Exeter. Thursday, 7th November 2013. 8:45 a.m.

Abrahams Fine Arts did not open until nine, but Cecilia had made sure they were there early, parked across the road, waiting.

At 8:50 a car came down the narrow, busy street and turned into the small parking area beside the shop. It was an Audi, A4 sedan, metallic silver, and the age identifier was 62.

"Gold star for Sister Chiara," Verity said.

A man got out of it and walked round to the front door of the gallery, which he proceeded to unlock. About five foot nine. Average build. Rimless glasses. Balding. Clean-shaven. Dark suit.

"Second gold star for Sister Chiara," Cecilia said as he disappeared inside. "Let's go."

It was a gallery full of wonders. As they entered a bell chimed and their quarry came forward with a pleasant smile.

"Good morning. Can I help you with anything, or would you just like to browse?"

"Actually," Cecilia said, as they produced their warrant cards, "we're police officers. I'm Detective Chief Inspector Cavaliere from Exeter CID, and this is Detective Sergeant Jones. You are Mr. Abrahams?"

"That's right," he said.

"We understand from the sisters at St. Boniface Abbey that you have offered to buy a painting of theirs. For £525,000."

He smiled. "Yes indeed. A beautiful piece! Gian Domenico Tiepolo! I should have enjoyed having it around for a while and getting to know it before I had to pass it on to Sotheby's. But the sisters have decided not to sell. In one way, I'm pleased. They have it in their meditation room you know, and it really belongs in a place like that, not in an art collection."

"That's more or less what Mother Evelyn said. Did you see the evaluation by Clark and Gregson?"

"Five hundred thousand pounds. Yes. I believe I have a photocopy of it in the office."

"So you were prepared to pay the sisters £25,000 more for their painting than the evaluation suggested?"

He smiled and shook his head.

"It was perhaps not the shrewdest offer I have ever made. But the work is beautiful and I thought the valuation on the low side. Clark and Gregson is a good, reliable firm, but inclined to be conservative—though to be fair, that's often quite a good thing in financial matters. Anyway, in this case, I believed I could cover what I laid out. An oil sketch by the same artist of Christ Calming the Tempest was sold by Christie's in Paris in 2008 for €720,500—that's just about £520,000, which is very nearly what I offered—and I was persuaded the sisters needed as much for the painting as they could get. They do much good work, and if they hadn't felt themselves to be in need of funds, I didn't think they'd have thought of selling at all."

"That was still generous of you, sir."

"Detective Chief Inspector, my grandparents came to Britain from Hitler's Austria in late 1938, after the Anschluss. They were penniless: a young Jewish couple in a strange land whose customs they did not know and whose language they hardly spoke. They'd only managed to get out of Austria at all because they had baptism certificates provided for them by an Anglican priest, a man called Hugh Grimes: *zichro livracha*! When they arrived in Britain, other members of the Church of England helped them until they could get on their feet. That, Detective Chief Inspector, is how my family survived. One does not forget such things. One *must* not forget."

There was a pause. Cecilia found herself thinking for a moment of Michael and his family, who had had their own stories of dealing with Nazi Germany.

"So," Abrahams asked, "is there some problem with the painting? I imagine you are not here asking about it out of mere curiosity?"

"It's been stolen."

"Oh dear." He sat down. "I am so sorry to hear that. And of course not many people knew it was even there. I was one person who did so I must be a suspect."

"At the moment, sir, we're just making routine inquiries. There are several possibilities."

"Of course you are welcome to search my premises as well, although of course even that wouldn't eliminate me unless I was a really very silly art thief."

"What would you have done with the painting if you were a very clever art thief, Mr. Abrahams?" Verity asked.

Abrahams smiled, lent forward, and put his fingers together.

"In the short term," he said, "I could have posted it to myself. Just to get it out of my hands, you understand, in case you came to search for it. So you probably ought to watch my postal deliveries for a few days, as well as searching my premises. But then over all I'd have two serious possibilities. One is, I already had a buyer before I stole the painting. In which case almost certainly I'd also have arranged for it to be by now well on its way, if not already delivered and being gloated over in secret by some collector of beauty who has more money and taste than honor. That way, I'd make a single hefty financial killing.

And in that case it could be years, decades — possibly though not certainly when the secret collector died — before the painting surfaced again."

"And the other possibility?"

"The other would be more complicated but the rewards would be greater. It would involve me either being or working with a painter who had fine art training and real ability. This painter would take the opportunity of possessing the stolen picture to study it. Really to study it! To live into it! Every brush stroke, every pigment! To enter the artist's mind, so far as possible. And then to copy it! And then perhaps to copy it several times! I am sure you can see where this is leading."

"You sell *all* your copies," Verity said, "pretending they're the original that was stolen?"

"Exactly! — to the same kind of secret collector as participated in the former scenario. Only this way, of course, I can accommodate several such collectors. It's really rather a stylish kind of crime, if a crime can have style. The buyers are happy so long as they think that they have the real thing — which if it's a really good copy may be forever! And if by any chance they do discover that they have a fake, what can they do about it? Since they bought it under the impression they were buying a stolen painting, they can hardly go to the police, can they? Those are the two possibilities, and I am virtually sure that one of them is what is happening to the sisters' painting."

Verity nodded.

"It seems then," she said, "that a copy can give you, or at least some people, as much pleasure as the original."

Cecilia gave a disapproving cough. But Abrahams spoke before she could.

"When I was studying in Paris I was sent on various occasions to the Louvre and the Musée d'Orsay to make copies as a part of my studies. What better way to learn, than to try to follow in the steps of a master? All art is in some sense imitation — mimesis — and to attend to something so closely that one can capture its essence is not to be a slave, but a disciple! And you are right: some copies have real beauty and can give great pleasure. So there's nothing wrong with making them, or even selling them, *just so long as you don't pretend they're the originals!* The moment you do that, of course they cease to be copies and become something else: forgeries. Fakes. Lies."

"You evidently have the skills to do this, Mr. Abrahams," Verity said.

"I do indeed! And I'm being as helpful as I can because I really hope you catch whoever did it and recover the painting. I didn't steal it and I've no idea who did. But until you catch them it seems to me I must be a suspect. I honestly don't see how you could *not* view me in that light. The bottom line, as the Americans say, is that art thieves get art dealers who try to be honest a bad name."

"What a delightful, interesting man!" Verity said when they were back in the car. "But is he for real? Do you think he's really trying to help, or he's just amusing himself by stringing us along?"

"If he is, he's good at it," Cecilia said. "And what he said about art theft was pretty well on the ball. By way of a crash course in what we're dealing with I phoned someone I know in the Met's Arts and Antiques Unit this morning, and he told me more or less exactly the same story. Anyway, let's keep our minds open to all possibilities, and go and see what Messrs. Clark and Gregson have to say for themselves."

SEVENTEEN

The Cathedral Close, Exeter, some fifteen minutes later.

The offices of Clark and Gregson, fine art auctioneers and valuers since 1876, were in the Cathedral Yard about twenty meters nearer to South Street than Harlow House—memorable to Cecilia as the place where she had made the most high profile arrest of her career.

They were greeted by an elderly man in a dark suit. They identified themselves, and explained their interest in a recently valued painting.

"Ah, yes," he said, "we have all sorts of specialists you know—coins, furniture, toys. But it's our Mr. Shale you'll be wanting to see for this one. He's on the top floor, and I'm afraid we don't have a lift. He says that way he and his staff keep fit and fewer people disturb them, which means he can get on with his work. I'll phone him and let him know you're on your way up. I'm sure he'll be anxious to see you."

In view of what had preceded it, quite why that last assertion would be true, Cecilia was not sure. But she let it pass and thanked him. Then she and Verity mounted four flights of dusty stairs to be faced at the top by a blue painted door with a brass handle and a neat sign that said: "Art Evaluation."

They knocked.

"Come in!"

They found themselves in a wide, lofty space that appeared to cover the floor area of virtually the entire building. The ceiling was covered with a lighting grid like a theatre, and everywhere there were long trellis tables covered with books, computers, more lights, cameras, and paintings. In the midst of this empire stood a pleasant looking, youngish man — Cecilia judged him to be in his mid-thirties at most — wearing a battered sports coat and flannels.

"Hello," he said, "I'm Edwin Shale. George told me you were on your way up. You'd normally find me in here with what we laughingly refer to as our staff — four other fine art nuts like me, only younger and prettier — but today they're all up at Rougemont Castle doing an on-the-spot evaluation. So I'm afraid it's just me. But I'll do my best. How can I help you?"

He addressed himself mainly to Verity, at whom he was looking with obvious admiration. Cecilia smiled inwardly. Evidently Edwin Shale had a penchant for neat blondes!

"We understand you recently did an evaluation of an eighteenth century painting of the Blessed Virgin for the Sisters of St. Boniface," Verity said.

"Oh, yes. Gian Domenico Tiepolo: in their meditation room. A beautiful work! The Virgin and Child. We did every kind of test on it. We're absolutely certain it's genuine, although there's room for a bit of disagreement about the date. Most of my colleagues want to date it around 1775 to 80, and they may be right. But I see similarities to a cycle of New Testament paintings that he did between 1786 and 1790. So I incline to think he painted it a bit later — maybe in the 1780s. In any case, it's a masterpiece. Personally I think it finer than anything else of his that I have ever seen. It has all his usual brilliance, but also something more. This Mary has looked upon the face of an angel. Her child is the Savior of the world. Frankly, when I saw it, I wept."

"Was this the only treasure you found at the abbey?"

"The sisters have some beautiful things—a good chalice and paten, and some excellent altar candlesticks. The Van Linge windows in the chapel are, of course, magnificent. But no, they don't, so far as I know, have any other treasure that matches the Tiepolo."

"Did you expect to find something like this when you began the evaluation, Mr. Shale?"

"We expected to find a painting of the Virgin and Child. There's mention of Bishop Phillpotts giving such a painting to the community in G. C. B. Davies' account of him, and if I remember rightly, also a reference in the DNB article about him. But neither mentions the artist or the date of the painting. So we'd assumed it would be a pleasant but probably fairly undistinguished Victorian piece. None of us dreamed of such a treasure as this! It's been a wonderful find! It would be fascinating to know how the bishop came by it. I understand that an older relative of his—someone on his wife's side—was at one time ambassador to Paris, so perhaps that's how it came into the family." Shale paused, and shook his head. "Sorry! I'm going on a bit. But then—those poor sisters! I saw on the news about that dreadful murder at the convent. That is so distressing. I believe I may actually have met the poor lady while I was there."

"I'm afraid there's also a problem with the painting, Mr. Shale."

"Oh really?"

"It's been stolen."

"Oh dear God!" He sat down abruptly. "Not many people knew where it was, we were among those who did, and we were certainly well aware of its value. And I suppose the theft and the murder must be connected?"

"At the moment, sir, we're just making routine inquiries," Cecilia said. "There are a number of possibilities. And we will need to interview the rest of your staff. Will they be here tomorrow?"

"They should be. And please feel free to look around here." He hesitated. "I suppose, though, that the painting wouldn't be here we had stolen it?" He paused again. "But then again, there's such a thing as hiding a thing in plain sight. So I dare say it might."

"People in the art world seem very relaxed about being suspects," Cecilia said. "That's not a feature we're used to in most of our investigations!"

He shrugged.

"It goes with the job," he said. "Fine art is big business. Investors see art as an alternative investment source for tangible assets. Which sickens me, because fine art ought to be about beauty and talent and passion but like much else in this country it's become about money. And one result of that is that art *theft* is on the increase. I was involved myself in such a case involving our London office only last year: a Renoir belonging to the Courtauld. One of those nudes he painted at the end of his career. In my opinion not at all his best work but still, a Renoir is a Renoir. So I suppose that's why I'm relaxed. I've been here before."

"Was it recovered?" she asked.

"Never a sniff of it. It may surface in time, if some greedy blighter that wanted it for his private collection snuffs it, and if somebody else — somebody honest — then realizes what it is. Or maybe someone will keep it to make copies and sell them as originals. That's been happening quite a lot in recent years."

Cecilia nodded. They all, it seemed, told the same story.

Verity had walked across the room and was looking at a row of paintings leaning against the far wall.

"These are beautiful," she said.

"They are, aren't they? One reward of my job is that I get to spend a great deal of time with beauty. These are mostly

English, nineteenth century. The Exeter Museum received a bequest, and it's all probably perfectly kosher, but the provenance of one or two of them is a bit iffy, and anyway they need to be evaluated for insurance purposes, so they've given us the job."

"This one's different," she said, pointing to a picture at the end of the row.

"Quite right," he said. "That's French, quite a different school. Do you like it?"

She looked for several minutes.

"I'm not sure," she said finally. "I think ... I don't really know how to look at it."

He nodded.

"An honest answer. Now at this point I could give you my brief but informative twenty-minute talk on the significance of this particular painter in the history of European art. Or I might just observe that we all like what we like and anyone who says we're wrong can shove it."

Verity chuckled.

"But then again," he said, "what you say about this particular painting is that you don't actually *know*. So may I try something?"

Verity nodded.

He picked up the painting, carried it over to a table, and propped it up so that it was facing her at about eye level. He adjusted several lights, stood back, made a correction to one of the lights, stood back again, and nodded.

"Right," he said to her, "now, you need to be here, I think, about six meters away from it—that's right. Now, look first at the mass of lights and colors in the center of the canvas. Focus on them. Try to feel those colors. Are you doing that?"

"Yes."

"Now, slowly, very slowly, move your gaze outward, take in the rest. Slowly. And try not to think. Feel."

He waited.

Suddenly Verity smiled, and nodded.

"It's wonderful," she said in quite a different tone of voice. "And that was extraordinary. Thank you."

"It's a pleasure," he said.

"Do you paint yourself, Mr. Shale?" she asked.

He laughed.

"Good heavens, no! Sadly, I've no skills that way. I'm just an art historian. I love the stuff, and I do know quite a lot about it. And I'm very good at sniffing out fakes. But I couldn't paint a decent picture to save my life."

There was a pause.

"I think, Mr. Shale," Cecilia said, "that we've finished, for the moment. Unless you have more questions, DS Jones?"

"Not for the moment, ma'am."

"Obviously, we may be back with more! But thank you."

As they were leaving, Verity turned back.

"And thank you," she said, "for helping me look at that marvelous painting."

He smiled.

"As I told you, one reward of my job is that I get to spend a great deal of time with beauty. Another is that just occasionally I have the incredible privilege of helping someone else to experience it. So for that, let *me* thank you."

"Another cool customer," Cecilia said when they were back in the car.

"Dishy, too," Verity said. "I could fancy him!"

"He evidently fancied you."

"Oh, well …" Verity colored slightly. "Anyway, he's certainly good at what he does. In fact he's more than good. He really helped me see that French painting. I mean, *see* it."

Cecilia nodded.

"That was very, very impressive," she said.

"What about searching all these premises, ma'am? Abrahams and here."

"The chief super told me this morning we can call on uniform from Exeter when we need to. But the fact is, for the moment I don't see we have anything on either that would justify a search warrant."

"They both said we could search anyway," Verity said.

"Which means either they aren't guilty, or they aren't worried because they've stashed it somewhere else. Either way, I don't as yet feel justified using time and resources for a search. But I do think we have more jobs for Joseph and/or whatever minions he can call on. I now want to know everything there is to know about Mr. Abrahams and Mr. Shale. And about the Renoir that got away — the one that was stolen at Shales's last place. I dare say the Met's art fraud people can help him with that. Although I also dare say he doesn't need me to tell him that."

"On it, ma'am." She hesitated. "Ma'am?"

"Yes, Verity?"

"I notice you didn't mention to Abrahams that this was a murder inquiry as well as an art theft?"

"I didn't mention it to either of them, actually. Shale made the connection himself."

"Why was that, ma'am? — that you didn't mention it to start with?"

"I suppose because as a general rule when I'm questioning people I try to get information rather than give it. What people then reveal they know can sometimes be very informative."

"And in this case?"

Cecilia shrugged.

"In this case I don't think I learned anything more from Shale's making the connection — other than that apparently he watches the news — than I learned from Abrahams' not making it—other than that apparently he doesn't. Did you pick up on something?"

"I don't think so, ma'am."

Cecilia looked at her watch.

"Lunch," she said. "I've arranged to meet Michael. Do you want to join us? I'm buying."

"Then I'm your woman," Verity said.

They met Michael at the Turk's Head in the High Street.

"We've just been interviewing all sorts of nice people," Cecilia said, "and they all seem terribly anxious to help the police and bring our art thief to book. And so far we can't tell whether they are lying through their teeth or not. But there are all sorts of things to follow up."

"By the way," Verity said, "do either of you know anything about Hugh Grimes? The chap Abrahams talked about? I'd never heard of him."

Cecilia shook her head and they both looked at Michael.

"Is this to do with rescuing Jews from the Nazis in the late thirties?" he asked.

"Apparently."

"Then as it happens, I do. He was a sort of British Schindler. When I was a boy he was quite a hero in our house: I think there were a couple of people in our synagogue whose grandparents had been saved by him. He was chaplain at the British Embassy church in Vienna in the thirties. I think perhaps he had some kind of diplomatic immunity. Anyway, he and his successor, another priest, rescued a lot of our people—maybe as many as eighteen hundred—more than Schindler, actually. He formally baptized them in the embassy church and then gave them baptism certificates. But he's never had much recognition for it."

"Why on earth not?"

"I think both the church and the Jewish community are

embarrassed about the baptisms — 'baptisms of convenience' — which I suppose they were. Personally, I doubt they embarrass our Lord. I think Grimes was a man with a generous heart. He saw something terrible and did what he could to help. He deserves more credit than he's got."

There was another pause.

"Talking of people getting credit, you seem to have fans at the abbey after your time there in Holy Week," Verity said. "Sister Agnes thinks you were '*wonderful.*'"

Michael smiled and shook his head in what Cecilia had come to know as a characteristic gesture of self-depreciation.

"O Lord! All I was doing was saying mass for them and giving them my dog and pony show about the Passion — basically filling in until the Bishop could turn up to be with them for the *triduum.*"

Verity nodded.

"That seems like a harmless enough occupation," she said, for the second time in two days.

Still, at least she didn't call him a turbulent priest.

EIGHTEEN

The road between Exeter and Edgestow, that afternoon.

They were on their way back to Edgestow, and Verity was driving.

Cecilia's mobile phone rang.

It was Tom Foss, from the laboratory.

"First of all, the room the picture was stolen from," he said. "There are shoe prints on the floor from the same Karrimo Tempo trainers as were worn by our second visitor in the orchard—so our guess that he was heading for the main abbey building was clearly right. There are also leather glove prints on the wall round where the painting was. With them it's the same story as before! If you can find the gloves, I dare say we can match them to the prints. And if whoever wore the gloves sweats in the usual way, I dare say they'll have his—or just possibly her, but I'll be surprised—DNA in them."

"Thank you," Cecilia said. "Verity, could you hear all that?"

"More or less," Verity said. "So we're not only looking for a stolen painting, we're looking for Karrimo Tempo trainers of the requisite size and leather gloves such as might have been worn by an art thief."

"You have it," Cecilia said. She turned back to the phone. "Anything else?"

"Very much so! The best is yet to be!"

"And that is?"

"Thanks to the brilliant and painstaking scientific work of our wonderfully talented forensic specialists, we've managed to find a tiny drop of human saliva on that posh cigar butt."

"And?"

"And there's a match," he said. "It's one Danny Kellog. He's got a bit of previous form: two counts of GBH."

"When was that?"

"1994 and 1996. Just recent enough to get him onto the data base!"

"And that's it? Nothing since?"

"Not until now."

"And is this our Mr. Kellog who had a run in with Mother Evelyn and owns a Rolls Royce and might give the town some money for a new clinic and lives in a big house in Blomfield?"

"According to our information, yes."

"But he's got an alibi."

"I'm just telling you what we found, Cecilia. We also found some grains of sand on the cigar, and they *don't* come from where we found it. Which looks as though it had been previously stuck in a sand tray to put it out."

"Curiouser and curiouser," Verity said when Foss had rung off.

Cecilia shook her head.

"Jarman and Wilkins are good lads," she said, "and I'm sure they did their best. But they're not all that experienced yet, so maybe they missed something. We'd better go and talk to Mr. Kellog ourselves."

She stabbed in another number on her mobile.

"Joseph! Good! Look, I know I asked you to be investigating Sister Barbara, and Verity's going to be coming on to you with some other things I need you to do for us. But just for this moment I'd really like you to drop every thing else and do us a rush job. I'd like you to see what you can find out about Danny Kellog—our rich Mr. Kellog on the posh estate. 40 Acacia Avenue, I think it is. Apparently he was done twice for GBH, in '94 and '96. What I want to know is exactly what those charges involved, and what he's been up to since. We're driving back to Edgestow now, and when we arrive we're going to pay him a visit. So that means you've got, oh, about an hour?"—she looked at Verity, who nodded—"yes, about an hour to find out what you can. We'll phone you when we get there."

"I am onto it, oh mighty one."

NINETEEN

Edgestow, later that afternoon.

They arrived at Blomfield at just after four o'clock. Acacia Avenue was wide and, in its way, gracious: handsome homes, built in the nineteen-nineties, set well back from the road, with spacious gardens and drives, and large double garages.

"Serious money!" Verity said.

Cecilia nodded.

"Let's stop here and call Joseph," she said.

"I'm sorry if it disappoints you," Joseph said, "but after an hour's research — which isn't much, I grant you — there's a not a lot against Danny Kellog, apart from his youthful follies, and even they don't amount to much. It's true he was arrested twice for GBH, but he was only convicted once, and even then he only got a suspended sentence and a fine. And from 1996 onwards, so far as I can see, he's been clean as a whistle. He's originally from south London — he grew up in Bermondsey. He got a job there in 1995 with a building supplies company called Belmont Supplies. He married the boss's daughter in 1997, and they've been running the business between them for the last thirteen years — since her dad retired in 2000. In 2002 they set up a branch in Exeter, in Grenadier Road, and then they moved down here to Devon to live. They still run both branches, and he goes up to London a couple of days a week."

"Building supplies?" Cecilia said. "That could be a cover for a lot of shifty things."

"This one isn't, not according to what I'm turning up. I can't find a thing against them. In fact it's all the other way. The word among my contacts and the reviewers is, Belmont Supplies is by no means the cheapest, but if you want to be sure the merchandise is top quality, it's honestly come by, and you're getting what you pay for, they're the ones you go to."

"Someone's been burying something," Verity said as they walked along the path towards the Kellogs's house. She pointed to newly turned earth in a flowerbed near the gate.

The door was opened by a nicely dressed, pleasant-looking woman in her late thirties or early forties, blonde and buxom.

"Good afternoon," Cecilia said, holding up her warrant card. "I am Detective Chief Inspector Cavaliere, and this is Detective Sergeant Jones. We're from Exeter CID, and we'd like to talk with Mr. Kellog, if he's in."

"You're lucky," she said in a London accent. "He come home from Exeter a bit early today. He's having his tea in the kitchen. Come on in."

They followed her through a pleasantly furnished house to a large, well-appointed kitchen, where a big, burly man in his shirtsleeves was sitting at a central unit drinking tea and eating a slice of fruitcake. French windows behind him faced onto a lawn, with woods beyond.

"Hello!" he said in the same London accent as his wife, "The Law, if I'm not mistaken!"

"Are we that obvious, Mr. Kellog?"

"You are to me, love. Don't worry. It's instinct where I come from. In the genes, you might say. You're both beautiful young women as well as being the Law, if that helps. Would you like a cup of tea? And a bit of cake? It's Josie's own, none of your shop-bought."

"Yes please, Mr. Kellog," Verity said. "I should love a piece of cake!"

"'Danny' will do, love. That's what everyone else calls me."

Josie was already pouring out the tea and cutting more slices of cake.

"Are those of your daughter?" Verity asked, indicating a cluster of framed photographs of a young woman on the wall by a window.

"Our Katie," Danny said. "Isn't she lovely? She's clever, too. Not like her daft old man. She's up at Oxford University!"

"Which college?" Verity asked.

"It's called Lady Margaret Hall."

Verity nodded. "And what's she reading?"

"Politics, Philosophy, and Economics."

"Ah! Now that's the way to the corridors of power," Verity said. "It's what the Prime Minister read!"

"Well, maybe," Danny said. "But our Katie says she means to come back and take over the business when we're ready for her to. Which is fine by us, if that's what she really wants to do."

"You must be very proud of her," Verity said.

Danny looked at his wife, and grinned.

"You could say that!" he said. "Though she was a bit of pain when she was a teenager."

"I can't imagine where she got that from," Josie said.

Cecilia began to have a distinct feeling that the situation was slipping out of control.

"All right, Danny," she said. "This is lovely, but for now, we'd like to talk to you about the night of the fifth of November. To be precise, we'd like you to confirm your whereabouts from eleven to one thirty-ish."

"When the little nun got murdered? I already told your

constables all about that—PC Jarman and PC Wilkins, wasn't it? Nice lads."

"That's right. But would you mind just going through it again for us?"

He shrugged, good-humoredly enough.

"All right. Josie and I were in The Great Western with friends. The Nicholses from down the road were there, and so were the Levovitches. Actually, I'd got to the pub about ten. I *was* intending just to have a pint and then come home. But then Josie called me on the mobile and said she was coming down with the others so we decided to make a night of it, what with it being Guy Fawkes and all."

"And you didn't leave your friends or the pub at all during that time?"

"Apart from a couple of visits to the gents I didn't leave the bar. Look—let's face it—loads of people saw us, and you're only questioning me again because you can't find any other suspects and you've suddenly found out I've got a bit of form."

Apart from the little matter of the cigar, he was right.

"But that was years ago," he pointed out.

"To be fair to you, Danny, it was very nearly twenty."

"And I've been a model citizen since. Daren't do anything else."

He looked across at his wife, who smiled reminiscently.

"He got a job with my dad," she said. "At our place in Bermondsey. 1995 it was—same year the Queen told Charles and Princess Di to get divorced. I was working in the office then, learning the business. Danny was a good worker but a bit of a tear-away. He had some horrible friends. My dad took him on because he liked him—well, partly actually 'cause *I* liked him—but it was risk. He'd already been in trouble with the law once, and then there was another punch up he got himself into a few weeks after he come to us. Well, I was pretty gorgeous back then—"

"Still are," Danny said.

"Shove it," she said, not unkindly. "As I say, I was pretty gorgeous back then and Danny fancied me like mad, an' as it happened I fancied him. So I told him straight, he could either keep going with his mates and getting into trouble, or he could have me. Not both."

"Guess what I chose!"

"Do you smoke, Danny?"

He grinned and looked at his wife.

"I'm allowed the occasional cigar if I've been very good," he said.

"What kind of cigars are you smoking at the moment, Danny?"

"He's going *slowly* through a box of Flor De Oliva Robustos," Josie Kellog said. "I got them for him for his birthday."

Cecilia sighed.

"Who's been digging recently in your front garden, Danny? In the flower bed?" Verity asked.

He frowned.

"Digging? Nobody, so far as I know. Have they?"

He looked at his wife.

She shrugged.

"Not me," she said.

"Then you won't mind if we go out and take another look at the flowerbed? See if there's anything there?"

"Help yourself," he said. "I'll come with you."

They walked out together with Danny and Josie to the flow-erbed. The patch of newly turned earth was obvious.

"Blimey," Danny said. "Who did that?"

"It wasn't done Tuesday," Josie said. "I know for a fact, 'cause I come home early, before it got dark, to cut back some of the roses for winter. I'm sure I'd not miss a pile of earth like that."

"What time was that?"

"A bit after four. But I suppose it could have been done any

time after that. I doubt we'd notice most of the time as we come
in and out, because we're generally using the cars and coming
straight up the drive to the garage."

Cecilia looked across at the drive, which led to the garage at
the side of the main house.

"I suppose you want a shovel?" Josie said.

"I hardly think we need it," Cecilia said, taking a pair of plastic gloves out of her shoulder bag and putting them on.

She knelt, and the first brush of her hands revealed blue cloth
buried beneath little more than an inch of loose soil.

"Blimey!" Danny said again.

Cecilia groped through the soil and pulled, and within seconds was holding up a blue cloth bundle. She opened it. It
was a pair of blue tracksuit bottoms wrapped round a pair of
trainers.

"Are these yours?" she asked.

"Never seen them in my life before."

"Then you won't mind if we take them away?"

"Be my guest," he said.

Verity, who had also put on plastic gloves, took the trainers
from her.

"What size shoes do you take, Danny?" she asked.

"Whatever fits."

"He takes tens," Josie said. "What of it?"

Verity tuned over the trainers.

"Nike LeBron Xes," she said noncommittally. "Size tens. I'll
fetch an evidence bag."

But Josie was beginning not to like the direction of this
conversation.

"Now wait a minute!" she said. "What's going on? Are you
lot are trying to fit my Danny up? How do we know you didn't
plant that stuff? Just because someone's had a couple of run-
ins with your lot way back when, you never leave him alone.
Anyway, like he's already told your constables. He was in the

pub with me all the time you're interested in. And so were a load of other people. So he couldn't possibly have done it."

"Would I be right, Danny," Cecilia asked, "in saying that you had a row with one of the sisters the day before the murder?"

"Oh *that*! I couldn't believe it! She ran into the back of my parked car and then when I went out to see what had happened she starting going on at me like it was *my* fault. I got irritated, I admit it, and I told her to get lost. I said I'd report the damage she'd done to my insurance company and she could pay for the repairs."

"And did you?"

"No, of course I didn't. It was only a scratch and I don't want the old bat's money. I'll just get the dealer to fix it next time it goes in for service. But like I said, I *was* ticked off at her going on at me like it was my fault. Nun or no nun, she should have been saying sorry to me, not the other way round. But just because I was ticked off at her doesn't mean I went and murdered one of her mates!"

Again Cecilia sighed.

"No," she said, "I can see that."

"Well that's very kind of you," Josie said sarcastically.

"My problem is, I've also got two pieces of evidence connecting you with the crime scene on the night of the murder — one is a Flor De Oliva Robusto cigar stub with your DNA on it that the scene-of-crime officers found."

"*What*? How the hell did that get there?"

"If it wasn't you that dropped it then I've no idea. The other is these trainers, which look like an exact match for trainers the killer wore."

"For God's sake, I don't care what you've found — "

"Or say you've found," Josie Kellog said.

" — I haven't killed anyone! Look, we've got a good life here. And you've seen the pictures of our Katie. Do you think I'd go and do something that would make her ashamed of us? Just because I'd had a row with some old lady?"

"Can either of you think of anyone who'd *want* to fit you up for this?" Cecilia asked.

"You mean apart from your lot?" Josie said. "No. We don't mix with that sort of people."

Cecilia looked at Danny.

"Not any more, I don't."

She looked at them both for a long moment.

"For what it's worth," she said finally," — and I'm breaking a personal rule even to say this to you — I believe you. If I didn't, I'd be arresting you on suspicion of murder. As it is, so far as the neighbors are concerned, for the moment you've merely been assisting us with our inquiries — as will every other house in the street, starting with the one opposite, to see if anyone saw somebody burying something in your front garden. One thing, though, until we've sorted all this out, don't leave Devon without letting us know, will you?"

Making good on Cecilia's word, she and Verity went across immediately to the house opposite, where they spoke with Mr. and Mrs. Gordon, an elderly retired couple, former journalists, who seemed eager enough to help, but had apparently seen nothing, heard nothing, and knew nothing.

"A lot of people would say the evidence against Kellog does look pretty damning," Verity said, when they were back in the car.

"I know," Cecilia said. "What would you say?"

"A bit *too* damning, actually. Too easy!"

Cecilia nodded. "That's my problem. If we'd had nothing but the cigar, I'd probably have pulled him in. But the trainers and tracksuit *as well*? Neatly but lightly buried at the front of the house where we practically fall over them? Despite the fact there's a back garden with woods beyond where you could hide an elephant? My instincts and my common sense tell me Josie's right. This is a fit up."

"Someone from Danny's past?"

"Maybe." Cecilia looked at her watch. "I said we'd meet with the others about now in the incident room. Let's go!"

TWENTY

St. Boniface Abbey, the incident room, later that afternoon.

They met at five with PCs Jarman and Wilkins and Joseph in the incident room. They told the story of the day.

"Jarman and Wilkins, I'll need you to check the rest of the houses in the road," Cecilia said. "You could do that tomorrow. See if anyone's noticed anything or anyone in the Kellog's garden over the last day or two."

The two PCs nodded, and looked at each other.

"On it, ma'am."

"And Verity, you and I need to sift Danny Kellog's alibi further: make sure it's really as good as it sounds. Just in case we were seduced this afternoon by south London charm."

"That and Josie's fruitcake," Verity said.

Cecilia nodded.

"We're passing the trainers and tracksuit over to forensics—yes?"

"Already done, ma'am."

"He says he's never seen them in his life before. Obviously, if forensics finds any trace that he *has* handled them, then south London charm or not he's right back in the frame."

She sat back and looked round the group.

"So, what else have we got?"

"I'm having a problem with Sister Barbara," Joseph said, "or rather with her former existence as Alice Hermione Walker."

"What kind of problem?"

"She certainly worked at a bank, as Mother Evelyn said— the Midland Bank as it was then, now HSBC. She joined them in 1990 and worked for them for three years until she decided to join the order here. She also had a bank account—with the Midland, naturally enough—which was opened in 1990. Her salary was paid into it. She had a three-bedroomed council flat in Paddington, also since 1990. All that's perfectly straightforward and clear, and everything checks out. The problem is, I can't find anything about her *before* 1990. Not a thing. I can't find her schools, anything about her education, where her family lived, anything. I can't even find a record of her birth. It's as if she didn't exist before then. As if she just suddenly came into being."

"Like Pallas Athena leaping fully armed from the head of Zeus!" Verity said brightly.

Joseph rolled his eyes at the ceiling, but otherwise did not respond.

"But doesn't her file give you a list of the schools she went to?" Cecilia said.

"It does, and it's useless. It says she attended St. Michael's School, Star Street, in Paddington from 1973 to '77: but that can't be true because that school was closed in 1972. Then she's supposed to have been at St. Marylebone Church of England School for girls from 1977 to 1985, which might make sense in terms of her becoming a financial wizard, because one of their specialties is maths and computing. But they have no record of an Alice Hermione Walker attending there between those years or any other time. I'm not blaming the sisters for not checking any of this. They'd no reason to be interested in where she went to school. But the fact is, that part of her file appears to be a complete fudge."

"If she became a nun, surely she must already have been attending some church?" PC Wilkins asked.

"She was. That's in the file. She was attending St. James, Sussex Gardens. And this time it's accurate. I talked with their assistant priest this afternoon. He was very helpful and checked the parish records for me. According to those, Alice Hermione Walker started attending in 1990 and got confirmed the same year. The notation in the register says she had no baptism certificate and didn't know if she'd been baptized or not, so the then vicar conditionally baptized her. Then in the register for 1993 there's another note about her joining the community at the Abbey of St. Boniface in Devon and going off the St. James electoral roll. So while the sisters didn't bother to check her schools, it looks as though they *did* get in touch with her priest and the church. Which is all perfectly fine as far as the church is concerned, but still doesn't get us back before 1990."

"It sounds to me as though Alice Hermione Walker wasn't her real name," PC Jarman said. "Maybe she was hiding from someone."

Cecilia nodded.

"I think you may well be right, constable. Or more likely, someone was hiding *her*. Someone influential."

"Why do you say that?" Joseph said.

"Because a single woman living by herself in London would be very unlikely to be allocated a three-bedroomed council flat. It would be unlikely now and I suspect it would have been even more unlikely in 1990. Which suggests to me that she had a *very* serious player on her side!"

"I suppose the next thing," Joseph said, "is for me to try and find if anyone's around who remembers her at the bank, or anyone on the council who knows how she got the flat. It's going to be a job, though, after twenty years."

Cecilia nodded. Things were beginning to come together. They were asking questions about a woman who more than once, according to their information, had expressed concern about family and what family could do to you, yet apparently had no family, and no past. No doubt there were several possible explanations for that, but at the moment she was struck by one possible explanation in particular.

She looked at Joseph.

"Yes, it will difficult to find people who remember her, after all this time. But there may be a quicker way. I think perhaps I know what this means. I need to make a phone call. Let's take a break."

Cecilia's call caught Chief Superintendent Davies as he was leaving his office in the Heavitree Police Station.

She told him her suspicions.

"You could be right," he said. "Let me make a call and get back to you as soon as I can. But that may be a while. Keep your mobile on!"

On her way back to the incident room, Cecilia met Mother Evelyn, and they walked a few meters together.

"By the way, Mother," she said, "did you have something of an altercation with Mr. Danny Kellog the other day?"

"Oh yes, I did!" Mother Evelyn said. "I feel so ashamed about that. I was quite in the wrong. I don't know what got into me. I was tired and our brakes aren't as good as they ought to be and I clipped the back of his beautiful car. But then his car, even with a scratch on it, looked so big and beautiful and shiny, and ours so small and dented and sad, and I suppose I was tired and I just lost my temper. But I was quite in the wrong. I would go round to see him and apologize, but he's going to insist we pay for the damage—as he's quite within his rights to do, of course—and it would look as if I were trying to persuade him to change his mind, wouldn't it? So I don't feel I can."

"I rather think," Cecilia said cautiously, "that Mr. Kellog is not intending to pursue you for the damage to his car."

That was, she reflected, a pathetically feeble paraphrase of Danny Kellog's "I don't want the old bat's money," but surely conveyed the general sense?

"Really? You don't think he's going to report it to his insurance company, then?"

"I don't believe so, Mother. I think it's quite likely that 'no further action will be taken' as we say in the police."

"Then you think it would be all right if I went round and apologized for my rudeness? You don't think he'd take it amiss?"

"I can't speak for him, obviously — but so far as I can see, no, I don't think he'd take it amiss."

"Then I shall."

"Good. There is just one other thing, though."

"Yes, Chief Inspector?"

"As a personal favor to me Mother, before you or any of the other sisters take that car out again, see that you get the brakes fixed!"

TWENTY-ONE

Gloucester Terrace, Edgestow, some hours later.

It was indeed a while before the chief superintendent got back to Cecilia.

She had ended her meeting with her colleagues, eaten a light supper at The Great Western, and returned to Mrs. Abney's when finally he called her — at just before a quarter to nine.

"Sorry it's taken so long," he said. "They were *very* cagey. They won't discuss anything over the phone, or use emails, or anything like that. Of course, the fact that they're in the middle of a massive re-organization doesn't help. Anyway, I finally got somewhere. You and I are to present ourselves in person, with ID, at 10:00 a.m. tomorrow at 1-6 Citadel Place, and someone called Commander Ian Salmon will see us. I've got us booked on the 6:52 to Paddington, which gets in at 9:00. I'll meet you tomorrow morning at Exeter St. David's in the booking hall at 6:30. All right?"

"Yes, sir."

1-6 Citadel Place. London. Headquarters of the recently established National Crime Agency, whose central bureau had among its responsibilities oversight of the United Kingdom Protected Persons Service — in short, witness protection.

Cecilia smiled.

She had noticed before that Chief Superintendent Davies was not one to waste his time with people in the middle. This, it seemed, was no exception. They were going straight to the top.

She called Verity.

"As you've probably guessed," she said, "there may be more to all this than we've realized."

"I was beginning to figure that out. I take it we don't mention possible details over the phone?"

"No. But here's the thing. I've talked to the chief super and he's talked to someone in London and as a result of all that he and I've got to go up there tomorrow morning. We're catching a train at the crack of dawn from Exeter. Actually, it'll be before dawn. I'm going to leave Edgestow now, I think. I'll go home for the night. That way at least I'll wake up in the right city. And I dare say Michael or Papa or Mama will drive me to the station."

"Right."

"So that means you're in charge down here, Verity. There's obviously plenty to do. I expect to brief you and the others on everything the chief super and I find out as soon as I get back. This could open up a whole new line of inquiry."

"No worries, ma'am, I'll see we get on with things. And you drive carefully. You've already had a long day."

It was just after ten thirty when Cecilia reached the outskirts of Exeter. The roads were quiet, almost deserted, and within minutes she had passed St. Mary's Church and was turning into the rectory drive.

The big Victorian house stood dark and silent. Evidently, everyone was having an early night.

Inside, on the second floor, there were gentle snores from her parents' bedroom.

From the-half open door to Rachel's bedroom Figaro emerged, tail waving, greeted her briefly, and then returned. Cecilia peered in. The child was asleep. She stood in the doorway for several minutes, and as her eyes adjusted to the dim light watched her daughter's gentle breathing, hair dark against the pillow, long lashes soft against her cheek. She longed to enter the room and touch her, but resisted the impulse. It would not be fair to wake her. So she stayed where she was and drank in the moment, while Figaro returned to his bed and, with a dreamy goodnight thump, went back to sleep.

"It's you!" Michael said as she slid down beside him in the sheets.

"Were you expecting someone else?"

"You might have found me in the arms of another woman," he said sleepily. "Then what would you have done?"

"Killed you both, of course. I'm a southern Italian."

"Just as well you didn't then. I'm sure that would have messed up your pension eligibility."

"Probably. The thing is, there seem to be unexpected complications with this murder we're investigating—as if a murder wasn't bad enough! Anyway, I've got to go up to London tomorrow with the chief super. I'm to meet him at the station—at St. David's—at six thirty a.m. Would you take me?"

"Yes."

"I'm sorry I woke you. I was trying to be quiet."

"That's all right. Actually, I'm starting to feel quite wide awake now."

"So I observe." She giggled. "Trust me! I'm a detective. I notice these things."

TWENTY-TWO

1-6 Citadel Place, London. Friday, 8ᵗʰ November.

It was a fresh, bright morning, everything on their journey to London left when it was supposed to leave and arrived when it was supposed to arrive, and Cecilia and Chief Superintendent Davies reached their destination in Citadel Place promptly at 9:55 am.

"Let's hope the National Crime Agency is as punctual as we are," Davies said as they approached the entrance. "Olwen's making steak and kidney pie tonight, and I don't want to be late for it."

The NCA *was* punctual.

The IDs of them both were checked courteously but thoroughly, after which they were shown into a more or less featureless office containing a picture of the Queen, a desk, a computer, three chairs, and not much else. There they were offered coffee or tea.

Cecilia took the tea, not because she expected it to be much good, but because she was thirsty.

A man entered and introduced himself as Commander Ian Salmon. Tall. Upright. Dark blue Savile Row-ish suit. Guards tie.

Smooth. Very smooth. Not Cecilia's type at all. Commander Salmon was probably a very slippery fish.

She stifled a giggle, embarrassed by the awful joke even though she had not actually made it, and as a result spluttered ungracefully into her tea.

The two men gazed at her.

"Er, are you all right, Detective Chief Inspector?" Commander Salmon asked. "Can I get you something? A glass of water? The tea and coffee here are pretty dreary, but I'd hate to think they were actually causing pain."

She warmed to him slightly.

"No," she said smiling, "thank you. Just a tickle in the throat! I'm fine. And the tea is …" she hesitated, torn between honesty and good manners—"… perfectly acceptable," she concluded.

"Well," he said, "if you're sure. Just ask if you change your mind." He sat behind the desk and placed a manila folder on it. "Now—you need to know about Alice Hermione Walker. And the first thing to say is, you were quite right. That wasn't her real name and she was under witness protection."

Fat lot of good it did her, Cecilia reflected.

"And now she's dead," the chief superintendent said bluntly.

The commander grimaced, and nodded.

"Yes," he said. "And frankly, Chief Superintendent, that could be our fault."

He sat back in his chair.

"I won't beat about the bush," he said. "We all know there have been some disastrous leaks and cockups in witness protection over the last few years, which is why the minister made her famous press release in December 2012, and why since then we've had all this organization and reorganization and extra screening put in place, all of which one *hopes* will make things better. What happened to this poor woman, Sister Barbara, may be a result of one of those leaks. Or may not. I honestly don't know, though I will try to find out. What I hope *will* be immediately useful to you in your murder investigation is if I tell you what we *do* know so far. Does that make sense?"

They both nodded.

"Right. Her real name was Ariana Maria Morina."

"Morina!" The chief superintendent reacted immediately. "I was a young copper in my first year—but I definitely remember the Morina family! God, were we glad to see that lot get nailed!"

Salmon nodded.

He looked towards Cecilia.

"You'll still have been a little girl, so you probably won't remember the Morinas—not unless you took a quite precocious interest in crime, but," —he pressed a key on the computer, and then swung the screen round to face her—"this was Ariana at nineteen years' old, when she was famous."

Cecilia found herself looking at a young woman with strong, rather striking features. Her hair was long and dark, and she was not wearing glasses or the habit of a nun. But those strong features had changed scarcely at all in the ensuing twenty-three years, and even if Salmon had not told her, there would have been little doubt in Cecilia's mind. This was the woman whose photograph was in the file. This was the woman who became Sister Barbara.

She looked at Salmon, and nodded.

"That's her," she said.

"The Morinas," Commander Salmon continued, looking directly at her, "were a criminal family. They moved here to London from Albania in the late forties. But they didn't come into prominence until later—the late seventies—the next generation blossoming no doubt in the warm sunshine of freedom and democracy." He gave a half smile and shook his head. "Anyway, suddenly, within a few years, they were into everything, and on a grand scale—drugs, the sex trade, protection, and of course murder. For a time they just about ran London's crime world. They were powerful in part, I think, because although they were brutal they rewarded loyalty.

Therefore they attracted loyalty. They were finally arrested by the Metropolitan police in 1989 after an investigation and surveillance that had taken over a year — and, incidentally, cost a fortune."

He pressed a computer key, and Cecilia found herself looking at a row of mug shots.

"There they are. From left to right you've got Jakov Morina the grandfather, and next to him Armend and Pjeter his sons. Next are Armend's three sons, Jakov and Rnor — identical twins, they are, as you can see — and then on the right Shpend, his youngest. Finally on the right you have Ervin Shala, also Albanian, not a member of the family by blood, but heavily involved in their activities."

Cecilia looked at them and nodded. Strong, dark faces, especially Jakov and Armand. She could see the resemblance to Ariana.

"What about women in the family?" she said. "I take it the Morina men didn't manage to breed by themselves?"

Salmon smiled.

"They didn't," he said. "Though mostly — there was one exception — the women don't seem to have had much to do with the business. In that respect the family seems to have been somewhat old-fashioned. Which I dare say is the reason why none of the women were ever charged with anything. Anyway, here they are."

He pressed another key. And now Cecilia found herself looking at shots of women.

"Again, from left to right. Ariana, Jakov's wife, who died in 1993; Lule, Armend's wife, who died in 2008; and Mirela, Pjetor's wife — she seems still to be alive although she's moved abroad. Costa Rica. She and Pjeter produced girls: so next to her on the screen is Ariana, their eldest daughter, whom you've already seen, who was born in 1970, and then to the right of her you see Mirela and Lule, twin sisters born to Mirela and Pjetor in 1978. So far as I know they're both living in Costa Rica with their mother. And finally Valdete Shala, Ervin Shala's wife. She died last year."

"What about wives for the younger Jakov and Rnor?"

"They've never married. Neither has Shpend — or at least, if he has, he's managed to keep very quiet about it."

"So — the men you showed me in the first set of mug shots were all charged?"

"Right. The trial lasted eight weeks and resulted in six convictions. Grandfather Jakov, his sons Armend and Pjeter, and their friend Irven Shala were all given life, without the option of parole. Jakov and Rnor the twins got thirty years apiece. Shpend got twenty. And the chief prosecution witness was Ariana Morina."

Davies nodded.

"She blew the lid on everything. At one point her grandfather had to be restrained from shouting at her in the court."

"And she's the woman who afterwards became Alice Hermione Walker."

"And then Sister Barbara of the Order of St. Boniface."

"And who's just been murdered," Cecilia said.

"A fact which had not escaped me," Salmon said. "Now, let me tell you a few more things about her that may or may not be relevant. First: you'll remember that when I said the women in the family didn't have anything to do with the family business, I also said there was one exception. That was Ariana. It seems she had a brilliant head for figures. The brief given to the Crown Prosecution Service described her as having carried out financial work for the family, done their bookkeeping, so to speak. Through that she'd gradually become aware of what the family was involved in, and was appalled by it. Finally it was all too much for her and she went to the police."

He paused for a moment, and then continued.

"That was probably true as far as it went. But it was hardly the whole truth. I've been looking at some other files on the investigation—files that didn't go to CPS—and it's quite obvious that Ariana had also been directly involved in some of the family's criminal activities. I'm not saying this to blacken the woman's character. I honestly can't imagine how someone could grow up in a family like that and *not* be involved in criminal acts. Anyway, she'd surely acted as courier on a couple of occasions. And she was almost certainly involved on one occasion in killing a member of a rival gang: got him to a hotel room in Frankfurt where one of her brothers shot him."

Cecilia drew in her breath sharply. That made sense of what both Michael and Sister Chiara had heard from her. *What if they'd persuaded you to do terrible things?* And, *families would ask awful things of you.* It also made sense what Mother Evelyn remembered her saying: *she couldn't even consider a vocation to the priesthood.* If she'd been involved in such a killing as Salmon described she might well feel that.

"I tell you this," Salmon continued, "simply because it *may* be relevant to her death, and you won't find any of it in the file that was presented to the Crown Prosecution Service—because, of course, for better or worse, CPS won't touch with a barge pole anything that looks like a plea bargain. If they'd been given a report of Ariana Morina's crimes, she'd have had to be tried for them. So the report omitted them. And for what it's worth, as I've read through the files I've become convinced she genuinely *had* turned against what her family was doing—become revolted by it. So to that extent, the brief the CPS received was correct." He pursed his lips and paused. "I dare say she made it clear she couldn't testify against her family if she had to do time herself. I imagine she was terrified of what would happen to her if she did. She'd have reason to be—if she'd gone to prison, they'd have had her killed."

"As it looks as if they did eventually, anyway," Cecilia said.

"Precisely, Detective Chief Inspector. Now, what do you propose to do with all this information?"

"Find out everything I can about this lot, sir," — she gestured toward the computer — "especially where they all are now. And then I want to interview them."

"Good," he said. "I thought you might. So this may save you some time and your staff some work. Everything we've got is in here."

He slid the manila folder over to her.

"I'm afraid," he said as he did so, "that you won't be able to interview Jakov Morina, not unless you dig him up. He died in the prison hospital at Belmarsh on the second of September: nothing spectacular or suspicious about it, so far as I can see, just general old age and decrepitude. Ervin Shala is also dead — died in Belmarsh in 2008. Again, nothing suspicious or spectacular. But Jakov's sons Armend and Pjeter are still banged up there, and so are Jakov junior and Rnor, so you shouldn't have too much trouble arranging interviews with them. They're all Category A, of course."

"With that record I'm surprised they're even allowed to be in the same prison as each other."

"They weren't for twenty years. But they'd been fairly well behaved, so the Home Secretary gave permission on compassionate grounds in 2010, when old Jakov was starting to get sick. So long as they behave themselves, or appear to, I dare say they may be allowed to remain. And it's certainly convenient for you if you want to talk to them."

"What about Shpend Morina? He's served his term, hasn't he?"

"He got out a couple of years ago, and seems since then to have kept more or less below the radar. He did come to the old man's funeral. There are photographs of him there. And he hung around for a few days. You're going to have to find him — but there is an address in the file, which is the latest we've got."

Cecilia nodded.

"You'll also see," he added, "that there are some notes about the women members of the family."

"Yes, I'll need to talk to them if possible."

"That may not be easy. There are really only the three left that you looked at—Pjetor's wife and his twin daughters—and as I said, they seem to be in Costa Rica: an interesting and civilized country and incidentally—or perhaps not so incidentally—one of the few interesting and civilized countries with which the United Kingdom does not have an extradition treaty. But what we have on them is there."

"Thank you, sir," Cecilia said, shuffling the papers in the folder. "All this will be very helpful."

He smiled.

"The Police National Computer is a wondrous thing," he said.

She paused and frowned as something caught her eye.

"I see Jakov Morina's funeral was on the fifth of September," she said, looking up. "At Kensal Green Cemetery. I wonder if there was anything about that on national news? On the BBC?"

Salmon shook his head.

"I'm afraid I don't know," he said.

"I do," Davies said. "Just a short item: I noticed it particularly. As I told you, I was a young copper when Jakov was in his prime. So there was no way I wouldn't sit up when I saw the old rogue had finally gone to meet his maker."

TWENTY-THREE

Citadel Place. About 11:15 a.m.

Outside in Citadel Place, Chief Superintendent Davies looked at Cecilia.

"Well," he said. "Was it worth it? Have you got something useful?"

"Yes sir. I think so sir."

"Good. I mean—I realize that Salmon fellow is a bit fishy."

She looked at him in amazement.

"I can't believe you just said that, sir."

"Said what?" he said, and looked at his watch.

"Sir," she said. "I know you don't want to be late for Mrs. Davies's steak and kidney pie, but it's not yet twenty past eleven. So do you think we might just have time to pay a visit to Kensal Green Cemetery before we go home?"

"Now why," he said to the air, "am I not surprised by this request?"

"We can go on the tube back the way we came, sir. And then Kensal Green's only five stops past Paddington on the Bakerloo. We can do the extra bit in no time, and then get back to Paddington in minutes ... well," she hesitated, "not too many minutes."

"Detective Chief Inspector Cavaliere, simply as a matter of interest, do you carry a map of the *entire* London tube network in your head?"

"Not all of it sir, but I was with the Met for four years before I came back to Devon. Paddington Police Station was more or less home to me. And I got to know Harrow Road pretty well. And therefore the Bakerloo line!"

He chuckled.

"Of course, you were in the Met. I was forgetting that. All right, Cavaliere, let's go and investigate your cemetery. Actually, I can't remember when I last did any real police work. And if we're late getting back to Exeter—well, I'll just have to rely on you to explain it all to Olwen. Fortunately, she likes you."

Twenty-Four

Verity had passed the morning with PCs Jarman and Wilkins, checking door to door the houses in Acacia Avenue. The results were largely negative. No one had noticed anyone doing anything, suspicious or otherwise, in the garden of number 40.

She had lunch with Joseph in The Great Western, and then decided to go back to the Incident Room and look again at her notes. As she got out of her car in front of the main abbey building, she met Sister Chiara, who was with Dismas.

"Hello," Chiara said. "Dismas and I are going for a walk. Would you like to come?"

"Yes," Verity said. "I would."

They walked together, while Dismas sniffed back and forth, chasing imaginary prey and generally showing off.

"It's very odd," Chiara said. "He has the run of the whole grounds, and roams freely all over them all day and every day, but still he comes back regularly after Morning Prayer and in the early afternoon and expects one of us to take him for a walk!"

"They like to have a routine," Verity said. "I've noticed

Cecilia's Figaro is exactly the same. This or that is what we normally do, so they expect us to do it!"

"To tell you the truth, I find Dismas' determination to keep us all on schedule almost as comforting as the Rule," Chiara said. "There may be wars and rumors of wars, and some careless person may have put the abomination of desolation where it ought not to be, but Dismas sees no reason why that should interfere with his walk!"

Verity laughed.

"Exactly so!" she said.

They walked on, chatting amiably. They discovered that they had been up at varsity during the same years, although Verity had been to Jesus College, Oxford and Chiara to Cambridge.

"I noticed when we were talking earlier you spoke of 'poor Stephen Hawking'," Verity said. "Do you know him? He's a Cambridge man, isn't he?"

"Yes, he is," Chiara said, "but I didn't mean that I know him personally. I just meant that I feel sorry for him because of what I know about him. He's so terribly ill."

They walked on for a few minutes.

"So are you a fan of Hawking's work?" Chiara asked.

"Hardly a fan," Verity said. "Vaguely interested, would be nearer the mark. And I've only read the popular stuff. *The Grand Design* – the thing he did with the fellow from Caltech. The real physics is quite beyond me."

Chiara smiled.

"Me too!" she said. "And that's the only thing I've read."

"What did you make of it?" Verity asked.

Chiara pursed her lips.

"Obviously he's mind-blowingly clever," she said finally, "and yet if you ask me he's also a classic example of left-brain overkill. He assumes everything can be construed by analysis and calculation! If it can't be analyzed or calculated, it can't exist! – and that assumption blinds him to things that *I* think glaringly obvious. He says human beings are just collections of particles of nature, and can't seem to see that at most that's only saying what they're made of. Particles don't have consciousness, and we do. So how does that come about?"

"I don't think he thinks consciousness is very significant," Verity said.

"Which is another part of my problem. Surely there's a built-in absurdity in trying to demonstrate anything *rationally*—reason being surely a function of consciousness—when you also that assert that consciousness has no significance? Don't philosophers have a technical term for that?"

"Yes," Verity said. "It's called sawing off the branch you're sitting on!"

Chiara laughed. Then—

"Oh—and now I've thought of something. Do you mind if we change the subject?"

"Of course not."

"Well it's probably quite irrelevant, but this morning while I was getting up I remembered something that maybe you and DCI Cavaliere ought to know."

Verity found herself making the encouraging noise that she'd heard Cecilia make at such moments. Imitation is, she reflected, the sincerest form of flattery.

"It's about when you asked us whether we'd had any unusual visitors to the abbey," Chiara said.

Verity nodded.

"Well this wasn't exactly a visitor, but it occurs to me that on the day before Sister Barbara died, I went to the gate during the morning to get the post and I saw a car parked in the road outside—with someone in it. I went back about an hour later because I realized I'd left behind one of the knapsacks we put the post in—there wasn't much that day and I hadn't needed it—and I noticed the car was *still* parked there. It seemed odd. I mean, there's no reason why you shouldn't park your car outside our gate and sit in it if you want to, but then, there seems to be no particular reason why you'd want to, not for all that time. So I wonder about it. And it struck me you ought to know."

"Did you notice what kind of car it was?"

"I only saw it through the grill. But it was a dark red Mercedes C class—a recent model, I'd say."

"Could you see the driver?"

"Not really, just a silhouette. Of course it may all be nothing at all to do with what you're investigating. Just mere co-incidence."

Verity blew out her cheeks.

"It may," she said. "But then again it may not!"

TWENTY-FIVE

Kensal Green, London. Half an hour or so later.

Kensal Green Cemetery on the Harrow Road, established in 1833 by the barrister George Frederick Carden and inspired by the cemetery of Père Lachaise in Paris, was surely among the most impressive places of its kind in the world. Among many distinctions acquired over the years was the recently consecrated Christian Orthodox burial ground – the first time that Christian Orthodoxy had had its own graves in central London. The chief superintendent asked where Jakov Morina was buried and he and Cecilia were quickly directed to the place: a grassy mound marked with a simple tablet and a crucifix placed, in the Orthodox tradition, at the feet of the buried so that it would be the first thing he saw at the resurrection.

They stood by the grave for a few minutes in silence, and then went to the cemetery office. Chief Superintendent Davies produced his warrant card at the reception desk, and introduced himself and Cecilia to the young man on duty, a genial seeming fellow whose lapel badge identified him as Henry Alchin.

"We're wondering if you can help us with our inquiries, Mr. Alchin," the chief superintendent said.

"I will if I can, officer."

Davies looked at Cecilia, who produced the photograph of Sister Barbara and handed it to him.

"Do you recall ever seeing this woman here?" he said.

Henry Alchin took the photograph and looked at it for a moment or so, then nodded.

"Actually," he said, "I do. She came in to ask where someone was buried. It was quite some weeks ago, though. Maybe even a couple of months back."

"Do you remember whose burial she was asking about?"

"Oh, yes. It was Jakov Morina. That was a big Orthodox funeral, and we had a lot of people asking about it even before it happened — reporters, weirdoes, all sorts. And then on the big day itself there were lots of police here. They allowed his imprisoned relatives to attend the funeral, but they obviously weren't taking any chances or letting them out of their sight! Still, I do remember this lady. She wasn't actually here at the funeral, you understand. She must have been here about a week after it. A very pleasant lady, as I recall."

"I think," Glyn Davies said as they walked back toward the tube station fifteen or so minutes later, "that what's emerging from this is a classic pattern."

"Sir?"

"Well, it's certainly true that witness protection sometimes fails because of leaks. I'm glad Salmon didn't try to wriggle out of that one, and he's right to look into it in this case. But the fact remains — simple statistic — that witness protection most *often* fails because of the people being protected."

"Really?"

"Something draws them back to precisely what they're supposed to be running away from. Their old haunts or their old life style, a pub they used to drink in or someone they once knew. Then someone recognizes them and their cover's blown. I'll be surprised if that isn't what happened here. Ariana Morina went to visit her grandfather's grave and someone recognized her."

Cecilia nodded.

"And recognizing her wouldn't have been difficult," she said. "Apart from wearing glasses, she really hadn't changed all that much."

Davies nodded.

"So," he said, "you want to interview the Morina family next?"

"I do sir, as soon as possible. And I'd like to take DS Jones with me."

"Right. Fixing interviews with the ones in Belmarsh should be easy enough. My office can arrange that for you. Shpend, the one who's out, may be more of a problem. Let me talk to the Met about that. Let's find out if he's at that address Salmon gave us, then take it from there."

They managed quite easily to catch the 2:06 from Paddington to Exeter St. David's. Davies called Olwen on his mobile from the train, and Olwen was waiting for them in the Davies' car when they came out of St. David's station at a little after twenty past four.

They drove Cecilia back to the rectory.

"Now," the chief superintendent said as she got out of the car, "I'm not sure what you were planning to do this evening, Cavaliere, but so far as I can see you've been rushing about virtually without stopping for the last four days. So I expect you to take the evening off, and I don't want you to be back in Edgestow before noon tomorrow. DS Jones and Sergeant Wyatt are perfectly competent to cope with anything that's likely to arise while you're away, and quite intelligent enough to let us know if for some reason they can't."

"Yes, sir," she said meekly.

For their part, Chief Superintendent Glyn Davies and Olwen arrived home in ample time to do justice later in the evening to Olwen's steak and kidney pie.

Twenty-Six

"There's a call for you, sir," Davies's secretary said. "It's a Commander Salmon from the National Crime Bureau."

"Thank you, Mary, put him through please .... Good morning, Commander."

"Good morning, Chief Superintendent. I've news for you."

"That's good—at least, I suppose it is."

"Well, it's news. You'll decide whether it's good or not. The staff here has been through everything we've got connected with Ariana Morina, and the upshot of it is, we're pretty sure there *was* a leak from witness protection, back in 1990."

"Do you know who?"

"We don't have proof that would stand up in court—but yes, almost certainly we do know. I've sent you a file by courier with the name and some details, then you'll have to decide what you're going to do with the information. It should reach you mid-morning. I rely on your discretion—and Cavaliere's."

"Understood."

Salmon hung up. Davies at once stabbed in another number.

"Cavaliere, good morning! You're still at the rectory?"

"Yes, sir. I was just getting ready to leave."

"Right. Well before you get on the road, you need to come

into the station here. Salmon's sending us some information by courier he thinks we should know. It looks as if there was a leak, after all. The information should be here by eleven."

"I'll be there, sir."

The same, just after half past eleven.

Cecilia read for twenty minutes. Finally she sat back, and looked at Davies.

"Well," he said. "What do you make of it?"

"I must admit," she said, "as soon as I saw the name I thought the worst. I knew Bert Tern back when I was a PC with the Met in Paddington. In fact I knew him better than I wanted to. He was a DI. He was bright, actually. Had some good results. But he didn't like me and I didn't like him. More to the point, I always suspected he was bent. Obviously I was right."

Davies nodded.

"But you can also see why they can't use this against him in court," he said.

Cecilia nodded.

"I can," she said. "Far too much that's still far too sensitive. And Bert's nicely retired on full pension." She frowned. "The problem is, it only gets us halfway. It tells us Bert was involved with witness protection in '90. It tells us he was involved in setting up Ariana Morina's new identity. And it pretty well tells us he was on the take and it involved her. What it *doesn't* tell us is the one thing we really want to know. Given he leaked Ariana's new name, who was it he leaked it *to*?"

She paused.

"I see he's retired to a place called Mousehole. Not inappropriate. Maybe should be Rat-hole. But as it's in Cornwall, it's sort of in our patch, isn't it?"

"It's pronounced 'Mowzel,' Cavaliere, and yes it is in our patch — sort of."

"Well, sir, I think that DS Jones and I should go to Mousehole and pay him a visit. Maybe we can coax out of him what we need to know."

Davies raised an eyebrow.

"A less trusting man than I might wonder what exactly you mean by 'coax,' Cavaliere, although I dare say I don't need to know so long as you don't actually break the law. But yes, I agree. By all means go and see him. And take DS Jones with you."

TWENTY-SEVEN

Mousehole, Cornwall. Sunday, 9ᵗʰ November.

The sky was fresh and brilliant, there was a breeze from the sea, and seagulls were diving and calling. From somewhere they could hear a church bell.

"What a lovely place!" Verity said as she got out of the car. "I wouldn't mind retiring here myself!"

Sea Cottage was pleasantly situated, overlooking the harbor. It was a pretty little house, though the garden was overgrown and untidy.

Cecilia rang the front door bell. There was a jangling from somewhere within, and they waited.

And waited.

She began to think there was nobody at home.

But then sounds of movement came from inside, and after another minute the door opened to reveal a pallid, seedy-looking man wearing a tweed sports coat and a plaid shirt. He seemed shorter than she remembered and he had a slight stoop. But his eyes hadn't changed.

"Hello Bert," she said, "Long time no see!"

He stared at her for a moment.

"My God! If it isn't the dago wonder girl! PC Cecily! And you've brought a little friend! What the hell do you want?"

"It's nice to see you, too, Bert," she said. "Actually ..." She produced her warrant card. "It's now Detective Chief Inspector Cavaliere of Exeter CID, and this is Detective Sergeant Jones. And what we want is to talk to you about your spell with witness protection in the early nineties."

"Well I don't want to talk to you. *Detective Chief Inspector*? My God, the force must have gone to pot!"

"May we come in?"

"Not unless you've got a search-warrant."

"We don't have a search-warrant, Bert. But we do have an ongoing murder inquiry. So what we *can* do is phone local uniform and tell them we have reason to believe you have information that bears on it, and that you're refusing to assist us. And then they can come round in a big shiny police car with a siren and flashing lights and cart you off to the local nick in full view of all your neighbors. And then we can have a formal interview down there, with you under caution and the recording equipment switched on and a solicitor present to advise you and everything proper and by the book. *If* that's what you want."

"You always were a smug little cow, Cecily. Always acting like you were superior to blokes like me. I see you haven't changed."

"So are we going to talk here or at the nick? Your choice."

"Come in if you must. But this is a bloody liberty."

They followed him into a small sitting room that was well furnished but untidy, and stank of stale tobacco. Tern threw himself onto a sofa and gazed up at them.

"So what do you want to know? I doubt I'll remember much. It was a long time ago."

"Ariana Maria Morina. Witness protection. No way you'll have forgotten her. She was the Crown's key witness in the criminal trial of the year. All we want to know is, who did you leak her new identity to? And we know you did leak it, so don't let's waste time arguing about that."

He reached for a cigarette, lit it, and drew on it. His hands were shaking slightly.

"And why would I agree I even know what you're talking about, let alone implicate myself in something you obviously can't prove?"

"Because the National Crime Agency has been re-evaluating all the files on cases you were involved in during the nineties. And what's in those files has led them to put two and two together and think seriously about presenting their conclusions to the Crown Prosecution Service. So this might be a good moment for you to tell us what we want to know."

"No way!" he said. "There's bugger all in those files that could stand up in court."

Cecilia said nothing. She removed several copies of *The Ring* from a chair, sat down on it, folded her arms, stared at him, and waited.

"It's bollocks." He drew again on his cigarette. "They couldn't prove a thing."

She smiled slowly, and shook her head.

"You really are out of date, you know. I mean, it wouldn't be just the Ariana Morina business, would it? Think of all the other cases you were involved in. Criminology has got *so* much more sophisticated than it was in your day. DNA testing for a start! Are you sure you want to risk it?"

"You're bluffing."

"Detective Sergeant Jones," Cecilia said, without taking her eyes off Tern, "I think perhaps you'd better call local uniform after all."

"Yes, ma'am," Verity said, and pulled her mobile phone out of her bag.

"Wait!" he said.

"Yes?"

He hesitated.

"Off the record?" he said.

"Don't fool around, Bert. There are two of us here so by definition nothing you tell us is off the record. I'll say this—I'm not interested in *you*, or how bent you were back when you were supposed to be a copper. Not my department. Ariana Morina has been murdered, and what I *am* interested in is who did it. If you've got information that bears on that, such as who knew her new identity, I want it. If you withhold that information, that's a criminal offense. You could be charged as an accessory to murder."

"There'd also be conspiring to pervert the course of justice," Verity put in with that air of demure, innocent helpfulness of which Cecilia had long observed she was absolute master. "We could do him for that too, ma'am."

"Very true, Detective Sergeant Jones. So we could."

"Which also carries a custodial sentence," Verity added in the same helpful tone.

"Indeed it does, Detective Sergeant. Thank you for reminding me."

"Geeze," Tern said, looking at Verity, "by the look of you I'd never have thought you'd be as much of a bitch as she is."

Verity gave a faint smile.

"That's because you don't know me," she said.

"So, Bert," Cecilia said, "here's the thing. Are you going to tell us what we want to know, or not?"

Again she waited.

"It was the old man," he said at last.

"Jakov Morina? He was already in jail."

"Fat lot that meant. He always had contacts."

She nodded.

"I dare say that's true."

"Old man Morina wanted to know what was Ariana's new identity, and where she was," Tern said.

"And you told him, Bert?"

"I got the information to him."

"Despite the fact that fear of the Morina family was precisely the reason why she'd been given a new identity in the first place?"

He gave the ghost of a shrug.

"And you told nobody else?"

"No," he said. Then he added after a moment, "Of course, I never knew who else he told."

"No. Of course you didn't."

There was a pause.

"One of the Morinas is out by now," Verity said. "Shpend Morina, the youngest—he got twenty years and he's finished serving it. Did you know him?"

"I knew *about* him," Tern said. "We all knew about all of them. Everyone did. They were famous back then. But I never met him."

"What did you know about him?"

"Just the word on the street."

"Which was?"

"Well, he was a villain, wasn't he? Just like the whole family were villains. But everyone said Shpend was a really nasty piece of work. And that he fancied himself. He thought he was the next big man."

"So," Cecilia said, "you told Jakov Morina Ariana's new name and address. And what did Jakov Morina do for you in return?"

Tern hesitated.

"I want to know, Bert," she said. "And I will find out."

"I owed the bookies," he said. "They were threatening me. The old man got them off my back. And why not? She was just another little crook anyway. She should have been banged up with the rest of them. She deserved whatever she got. I was doing the world a favor."

Cecilia sat back and gave a half smile.

"Oh, Bert, Bert!" she said. "So *that* was why you sold her

out—to do the world a favor! Why didn't you tell us before? You really ought to write a book about it. Bert Tern's memoirs! *How I Saved England for Freedom and Democracy.*"

She gazed at him for a moment longer, then looked at Verity.

"Do you have any more questions for this man, Detective Sergeant Jones?"

"No, ma'am. I think I've heard just about all I want from him."

Cecilia got to her feet.

"Then I believe we're done here," she said.

She looked down at Tern.

"Enjoy your pension, Bert," she said, "the reward for all those years of faithful service. And don't worry about getting up, we'll see ourselves out."

As they left, Verity, who was following Cecilia, stopped in the doorway and turned back.

"You know," she said to Tern, "I think there's a reason why 'PC Cecily' used to act as if she was superior to blokes like you. It's because she was."

Outside on the doorstep in sunshine and fresh air they both took deep breaths.

"Has the National Crime Agency really been thinking about turning over those old files to the Crown Prosecution Service?" Verity asked as they walked towards the car.

"I imagine they must have thought about it."

"But is there really enough evidence in them to bring into court?"

"I doubt it."

"But I thought you said—?"

"I never said there was enough evidence."

They walked on in silence for a few more yards.

"Do you ever play cards, ma'am? Poker, or anything like that?"

"No. Why?"

"It's just that if ever you do, please remind me not to play against you!"

Cecilia smiled.

"There's a whole lot here that's still a complete mystery to me," she said.

"Yes, ma'am?"

"If Bert Tern leaked Ariana's new identity to Jakov Morina in 1990, and if the Morinas then took revenge on her, why on earth did it take them twenty-three years to get round to it? And how on earth does the painting fit into all this? Did they wait until they saw the chance to steal a valuable work of art and *then* decide to kill her while they were at it?" She sighed. "It still doesn't make any sense."

Twenty-Eight

Armend Morina looked, if anything, offended by the question.

"We took twenty-three years to get round to it, Detective Chief Inspector, and would have taken twenty-three more, because we never intended to 'get round to it' as you put it. I do not deny—even in here we have power and contacts. We can from time to time orchestrate events if we want to. But we did not orchestrate the death of my niece."

"And the Tiepolo Madonna and Child?"

"I know nothing of it."

And it really sounded as if he didn't.

Cecilia frowned.

With the governor's permission she and Verity had spent the best part of the day in Belmarsh Prison, and had interviewed in turn various members of the Morina family who were incarcerated there. They had heard from each more or less the same story. Armend, the eldest, was the last.

"So you're telling us that your father went to all the trouble of finding out his granddaughter's new identity, and it wasn't because he was out for revenge?"

"I am."

"But he was furious with her! He threatened her when he was in the dock!"

"And you are going to say that he was a hard and violent man, with a great deal of blood on his hands. Yes?"

"Yes."

Armend smiled and shook his head.

"But he loved Ariana," he said. "She was the apple of his eye. And he admired her. Do you know what he said to us once when he had us all together? When we were very young? He said, 'See Ariana here? She's only a girl but she's got more brains than the rest of you put together!' In the courtroom he shouted words of rage at her for what she had done to us, but he would never really have harmed her."

"Surely he felt betrayed by her?" Verity asked.

"Yes, he did, Detective Sergeant. But he also forgave her. And he was the head of our household. Vengeance was his right, if he chose it; and his also was the right to forgive, if he chose."

"But *why* would he forgive her?" Cecilia asked. "I find that extraordinary."

"*Because* he chose to! He told me once he understood why she had done it. He said she looked straight at him while she was in the witness box, defiantly, challenging him, moments after he had shouted at her. And in that moment, though he was angry with her, he was also proud of her, of what she had become. 'She is what I have made her,' he said to me, 'what I, at times, wish I had been myself. She did what she believed was right. She is a woman of honor.' So she was not to be harmed."

"Even you can't deny that such forgiveness is unusual?"

"My father was an unusual man."

Evidently he was, Cecilia reflected.

"I am but his shadow," Armend continued. "And I, for one, would not have disrespected his decision by questioning it."

"I'm not sure I can believe you."

"Detective Chief Inspector, I do not care whether you believe me or not. This conversation was not my idea, and if you think I am not telling you anything that you can believe, so be it. In that case, may I go now and stop wasting both our times?"

"No, you may not. And I'll decide when we're wasting time. So why do you think your father was so anxious to learn Ariana's new identity, if he didn't want to harm her?"

"I don't *think*, I *know* why. He wanted to know who and where she was so that he could protect her. That was the whole point. He knew there were those who would never forgive her. He knew what she had risked. And the family was absolutely forbidden to do anything to harm her. We all knew that. Do you know what is the problem with you and your kind, Detective Chief Inspector?"

"What is our problem, Mr. Morina?"

"You see everything that is bad about us, everything that breaks your laws. But you cannot see what is good, what is faithful, what is loyal. What just might transcend what you expect of us. Tell me, Chief Inspector, have you read the accounts of our trial?"

"I haven't."

"Perhaps you should. If ever you do, remember all those Mafiosi bosses, who are swaggering *capi dei capi* until they are arrested, and then in the dock become shuffling old men in baggy trousers, whimpering about their age and their liver and their dependence on insulin, hoping to get a lighter sentence! Then compare them to my father, who never appeared in court other than immaculate in an Armani suit, who did not flinch when sentenced, and who would have considered even an implicit request for mercy nothing less than a betrayal of honor. *That* was my father."

Cecilia gazed at him for a moment.

"And so," she said finally, "you didn't know anything about your niece's death until this morning?"

"On my life, that is the truth. And she shall be avenged."

Cecilia raised an eyebrow.

"It sounds as if you have some idea who the killers are."

His lips tightened.

"Clearly," he said, "they were people who did not respect the wishes of my father."

"So they would not have been members of your family?"

"I have told you, they were people who did not respect the wishes of my father. And I will tell you something else. If we get to them before you do, even though one of them were the son of my own begetting, we shall save the English taxpayer a great deal of money." He gave a faint smile. "So—if *you* know anything, why not give me a name? There will be no need for lawyers and judges and an expensive trial. Who knows? We might even get your missing Madonna and Child back! Win-win for everybody!"

"That's the second time in minutes you've made a threat, Mr. Morina."

He laughed.

"What are you going to do about it? I am in this place for life. Or are you God, Chief Inspector, able to force upon me another life so that I may serve more time?"

He leaned forward, and Cecilia was suddenly struck by the marked resemblance his strong, dark features bore to Sister Barbara's in the photographs she had seen.

"There are," he said, "police officers to whom I would have made such an offer seriously. And there are police officers who would have taken me up. I don't mean corrupt or greedy officers—I offered no bribe, you will note. I simply mean officers who see that sometimes what you want as justice and what we want may coincide. In which case life can be made simpler for everyone. But with you, Chief Inspector? No, with you I was joking. I know what I am dealing with. You have a love of law and due process that I find very English; and along with it a

certain passion that I find very Italian. I hope that in the end one
of us will find Ariana's killer. I rather think one of us will—but
in our own way."

"What do you reckon?" Cecilia asked Verity when they were
back in the car.

"For the most part I think they're telling the truth as they
see it," Verity said. "They're a brutal lot, but they seem to have
their own code of honor and they aren't without dignity."

"Armend in particular," Cecilia said. "If Jakov Morina was
anything like him, I can see why the family became so powerful. He's intelligent and he has charisma. There were moments
when I wasn't sure whether we were interviewing him or he
was interviewing us! And yet he says he's just the shadow of
his father!"

"Where that gets us in terms of solving Sister Barbara's
murder or finding our painting I don't know," Verity said.
"The Morina family's knowing who she was in her previous
life is starting to look like another open road that's turned into
a dead end."

"I don't agree," Cecilia said. "There's no doubt Ariana being
killed and the theft of the Madonna were parts of one and the
same operation, and what I've learned from today's conversations is that Armend has at least a pretty good idea who did
the killing, or thinks he has. But when I asked him if it could
or couldn't be a member of the family, he evaded the question.
Then suddenly he handed out all that stuff about 'give me a
name and I'll finish the job'—which was just a distraction, as
he virtually admitted in the next breath. All of which leaves me
wanting more than ever to talk to his son Shpend, the one that
got away, the one Bert Tern says fancied himself as the next big
man. I wonder if Shpend Morina's ever been to Edgestow?"

***

At Chief Superintendent Davies's request the Metropolitan
Police had indeed visited Shpend Morina's last known address
with an invitation to assist the police in their inquiries, but as
Commander Salmon had feared, they found him to be long
gone. There was, of course, no forwarding address.

"We've got the mug shot of him the NCA gave you," Verity
said. "We could try flashing that around Edgestow. Just on the
off chance he's been there and someone saw him."

For now, however, Shpend Morina's whereabouts remained
a mystery.

Twenty-Nine

St. Boniface Abbey. Tuesday, 12th November.

It was a fine, clear day with a hint of frost in the air.

The funeral and requiem for Sister Barbara were to be in the abbey chapel at 10:00 a.m. As was her custom when investigating a murder, Cecilia planned to attend, not only out of respect for the victim and those who mourned her, but also to observe the mourners.

The Bishop would preach and celebrate, and Father Carlton the chaplain was to assist. Mother Evelyn had also invited Michael to be present, and he arrived in his car at just after nine-thirty.

"I see you've brought your stuff!" Cecilia said. "Are you going to be doing something in the service?"

"I don't think so. I think Mother Evelyn just invited me because I know the sisters."

"Well, I'm going to the funeral too. So I wondered if you'd like to sit with me?"

"Absolutely!" he said, and put his alb back into the car.

"I love the light in here," she whispered as they entered the little church. "I suppose it's the glass."

"I think it *is* the glass," he whispered back. "It's rather special."

The little church was packed, not only with local people—
she recognized, among others, Jim Pettigrew and his daughter
Jennifer, Dick and Patti Posan, and (somewhat to her surprise)
Danny and Josie Kellog, who were talking with Mother Evelyn—
amicably enough, it appeared, since they were all smiling. So
surely Evelyn had already been to see them and made her apol-
ogy? There were also a number of outsiders present, as there
always is when there is a degree of scandal. Among these were
several reporters, most of whom Cecilia recognized. One or
two she did not recognize, such as two young women wearing
Associated Press badges with whom she saw Verity speaking.
Verity herself was immaculate as usual, today in her mourning
black: there was a woman who really knew how to dress for a
funeral! Joseph was nearby, on this occasion as immaculate as
his fiancée, in dark suit and tie, talking to Sister Francis. BBC
South West and the local independent television network had
sent teams along: but these, at the bishop's request, confined
their activities to filming and interviewing outside the church.

She and Michael were conducted—again somewhat to her
surprise, but she supposed it was because he was a priest—
through the nave to the choir, and there placed in the second
row of stalls, behind the sisters, who were in the front row.
Sister Chiara and Sister Agnes were directly in front of them.

The bishop celebrated gently but with presence, and his
sermon was a brief, graceful recollection of the departed sister
and a firm affirmation of Christian hope for resurrection.

Yet even that hope, he said, did not mean those who knew
Sister Barbara would not or should not feel sadness in the present moment. Nor did their duty to forgive those who harmed
them mean that there was not still a part of them that cried out,
"No! This should not be!" They had lost a woman who in the
world's sense possessed nothing. And yet, as many present—
including himself—could testify, every day she gave away to
those who came to her things infinitely precious: her time, her

attention, her counsel, and her prayers. If then they felt grief or anger at her sudden and violent taking from them, that was not something for which they need apologize. Not for nothing, faced with the world's evil, did our Lord say, "Blessed are those who mourn."

Benefitting from her vantage point in the choir, Cecilia was able discreetly to watch the congregation while the bishop spoke. She saw attention on the faces of most and grief on not a few. She saw nothing to make her think she was looking at Sister Barbara's killer.

The rite ended with the entire congregation accompanying the coffin to the sisters' cemetery and seeing it interred. The sisters, gathered around the grave, conducted themselves with dignity, although Cecilia could see tears on the cheeks of them all. Everyone present seemed moved. She noticed even one of the young women from AP wiping her eyes as she stood with other reporters on the fringe of the crowd.

It was only as they were walking back from the cemetery toward the reception that Cecilia allowed herself to relax for a moment from being the police detective, and in that moment to feel the impact of the bishop's words. She bit her lip, suddenly aware of her own anger at Sister Barbara's death. And she had never even met the woman! How then must those who had seen and known her feel?

"What's the matter?" Michael said.

She shook her head.

"It's just—well, you can be so busy trying to find the killer and doing your job, you forget just *why* you're doing it. But then when it comes home to you! Dear God, this was such a total bloody waste of what was obviously a wonderful woman. I *ought* to be angry."

Michael nodded.

They walked on for a minute or so in silence.

"Still," he said, "while I agree with you completely, I hope you won't give up altogether on your cool and rational side! We need people like you to stay calm. Otherwise the murderers would never get caught."

"Always assuming we *do* catch them."

"Oh, you'll catch them all right."

She smiled despite herself. His confidence in them was encouraging, even though in the present state of their investigations she wasn't at all sure she could share it.

They were overtaken by Father Carlton, resplendent in multi-buttoned cassock, *pellegrina*, and biretta. He turned briefly as he passed them to nod to Michael, who nodded gravely back. Then he flapped on ahead of them, full of affairs.

Cecilia gazed after him.

"'*A person and face,*" she said at last, "*of strong, natural insignificance, though adorned in the first style of fashion*'!"

"Ouch!"

"Jane Austen. Sorry! I know he's your brother in arms, or cassock, or whatever. But priests like him tend to have that effect on me."

Michael sighed.

"I'm afraid poor Carlton has that effect on a lot of people."

They walked on for a few more minutes in silence, now holding hands.

"So what's special about the glass in the chapel?" she asked.

"It was made by a Dutchman called Bernard van Linge, and it's surely what gives the wonderful light. He did it just after he'd finished Wadham College Chapel — and some people think St. Boniface's is better. I'm not sure. Wadham's east window is magnificent."

"It was lucky to survive the civil war, wasn't it? Didn't the puritans smash up windows with saints and things in them?"

"Yes, confound them! The Wadham legend is that throughout the war the college was lucky enough to be served by a bunch of crooks and timeservers who didn't give a damn who won just so long as they got left alone! At tricky moments they'd have a man posted in the tower with the king's flag in one hand and parliament's in the other, ready to run up either fast, according to whose troops appeared on the scene. I don't know if that's true, but it's certainly true that Wadham still has its pre-civil war glass."

"What about this place, then?"

"I dare say it wasn't important enough for anyone to bother about it."

"And clever enough to keep its head down?"

"Absolutely."

When Verity got back to her desk after the funeral, she found a message waiting for her. It was from Edwin Shale, the art specialist at Clark and Gregson's. Would she phone him back at his office, where he would be until five? And the number.

Intrigued, she phoned.

"Oh, thanks so much for calling," he said. "The thing is, I've got tickets for *Warhorse* in Plymouth next Saturday evening, and I wondered if perhaps you'd do me the honor of coming with me?"

"Oh!" She felt herself coloring. "I assumed this was you calling me about the case we're working on."

"No," he said. "This is me calling you to ask you if you'd go to the theatre with me."

"Well," she said, "that would be lovely. Only I think my fiancé would probably want to come too."

"Oh Lord," he said, "I'm such an idiot. I didn't realize. I do apologize—to you and to your fortunate fiancé!"

She laughed.

"There's certainly no need to apologize. I'm flattered. And although I won't go to the theatre with you, I don't see any reason why I shouldn't tell you that you've somewhat changed my life. By which I mean that after you showed me how to look at that painting when we were in your office the other day, I don't believe I shall ever look at a painting in the same way again. You've given me a beautiful gift, and I am very, very grateful."

"What a lovely compliment!" he said. "That makes me glad I telephoned you, even though you won't go to the theatre with me. Thank you! Goodbye, Verity. Forgive me—may I call you Verity?"

"Of course you may. Goodbye, Edwin."

THIRTY

40 Acacia Avenue, the afternoon of the same day.

"You lot again!" Danny Kellog said, though his tone was not unfriendly. "Josie!" he said over his shoulder, "The law's back! They must have heard you put the kettle on."

"May we come in, Danny?"

"We're in the kitchen, like always."

As they followed him to the kitchen, Danny said, "By the way—did you know your Mother Evelyn came round and apologized to me about the car? You could have knocked me down with a feather! Actually, she's not at all a bad old thing when you get to know her a bit. Josie likes her!"

Cecilia smiled.

"I'm glad you're friends," she said. "I think she's a good person. In fact I think all the sisters are."

In the kitchen, Josie was already filling the mugs of tea she then placed in front of them. She had, Cecilia noted, remembered that Verity took two teaspoons full of sugar and a lot of milk, whereas Cecilia just took a little milk. They settled themselves at the center unit, and Josie offered lemon-ginger biscuits.

"There's no cake today," she said. "He's eaten it all."

"I suppose," Danny said as they took their biscuits, "you want to hear me tell the story of Guy Fawkes Night over again, in case I get a bit wrong this time?"

But all the story of the night told over .... Not this time, though.

"No Danny, actually we don't. What we want is to know if either of you have ever seen this man."

She nodded to Verity, who produced a photograph from her handbag and passed it to Danny.

He gazed at it.

"He does look sort of familiar," he said at last, "but I can't place him. Can you?"

He passed the photograph to Josie, who looked at it for mere seconds and then said, "Hrrmph!"

"You've seen him, Josie?" Cecilia asked.

"Well no, not lately. Not round here I haven't and I don't want to. But I know who he is, all right, and" — to her husband — "so do you! That's Slimy Spend, from school."

"Slimy Spend?" Cecilia exchanged glance with Verity. This was not at all the answer they'd expected or hoped for, but it was certainly intriguing.

"That's what we called him," Josie said. "He's grown a beard and of course he's older, but I still remember his face. Shpend Morina — that was it."

Danny gazed at the picture again.

"Yes," he said, "I do sort of remember him now."

Josie laughed.

"You bloody well ought to, seeing as you beat the crap out of him. It was a fair fight, though," she added for Cecilia's and Verity's benefit. "At least, it was fair on Danny's side."

"It wasn't anything much," Danny said.

"Yes, it was. Would you two like to hear?"

"I can't wait," Cecilia said, settling herself in front of her mug of tea and her lemon ginger biscuit.

"Me neither," Verity said, enthusiastically if ungrammatically.

"Back then," Josie said, "we all went to Furzedown Secondary in the Welham Road. It's not there any more, been amalgamated. Anyway, everyone knew Slimy Spend in the top form, though you didn't call him that to his face: he was big, and he was a bully. And he didn't mind who it was he bullied, neither. Girls, boys, even if they were little, it was all the same to Slimy. Well, he called Danny's sister a tart, in front of everybody, and Danny told him to take it back, and he wouldn't, so Danny challenged him to a fight, after school, round the back, in the playground."

She paused, and drank some of her tea. A born storyteller, Cecilia thought.

"Well, everyone in the school knew about it. We all wanted to see Slimy Spend get his come-uppance, all of us except his little gang of toadies. And that was where Slimy made a mistake. He turned up round the back after school with his little gang, and I reckon he thought they'd all just join in and beat Danny up between them. He hadn't bargained on the fact that half the school came along to watch."

"I wasn't totally stupid," Danny said. "I'd taken along a few of my own mates, just in case he tried something on. But I must admit I hadn't realized half the school would be there either."

"Do you think the teachers knew about it?" Verity asked. "They must have, surely?"

Danny shrugged.

"'*Course* they knew!" Josie said. "Most of them were watching out of the top windows. They just turned a blind eye. They didn't like Slimy any more than we did."

"Well, what happened?" Cecilia asked.

"To start with," Josie said, "Slimy tried to cheat. Danny offered to shake hands before they started, and Slimy made like he would, and then tried to kick Danny in the balls!"

Danny chuckled.

"Luckily," he said, "I saw it coming and dodged. Never moved so fast in my life!"

"So then what happened?" Verity said.

"Oh, it was a terrific fight," Josie said.

"He was tough, I'll give him that," Danny said.

"Yes, but you were tougher — *and* he was a year older and he was bigger than you! Danny was wonderful!" she said.

"I thought you didn't approve of me fighting?"

"I don't, now you're a grown-up. But it was different then."

"So I take it Danny won?" Cecilia said.

"He won, all right. He had Slimy down on the ground at the finish with his arm up behind his back. 'Take it back, what you said about my sister! Say you take it back, or I'll break your bloody arm for you!' he said. And I reckon he would have, too, he was that mad."

"I don't expect I would of, really," Danny said. "Not on purpose, anyway."

"And did Slimy take it back?"

"Oh yes, he took it back alright!" Josie said. "He was almost crying with the pain. Well, no, he *was* crying. 'I take it back, I take it back,' he said. And then Danny let him get up. 'Don't you ever even dare speak my sister's *name* again,' he said, 'or you know what'll happen,' and then he turned his back on Slimy and walked off with his mates."

"So was that," Cecilia could not help asking, "when you first started to fancy Danny?"

Josie laughed.

"I'd fancied him for weeks! I dare say that was when I first *really* started to fancy him! I mean, I got a *serious* crush. 'Course it was all one-way. He was seventeen and I was thirteen. He didn't know I existed." She grinned. "It wasn't until I got Dad to let him come and work for us that *he* noticed *me*. I was twenty by then. And *then* the boot was on the other foot!"

"Still is!" he muttered.

"So why are you showing mug-shots of Slimy around now?" Josie asked. "Did he have something to do with killing the sister?"

Cecilia did her best to sound non-committal.

"We think maybe he can assist us in our inquiries," she said. She always felt something of a fraud when she said that, but given they hadn't a scrap of evidence even as to Shpend Morina's whereabouts on the night of the murder, what else was she to say? "Anyway, you've not seen him since school? And never round here?"

"No. And I'm sure I'd remember if I had. All I know is, I think he got sent to some posh college for a bit after he left Furzedown—of course the Morinas were loaded, we all knew that. And then of course everyone knew about it when he got banged up with the rest of them."

"Well that was a total surprise," Cecilia said when she and Verity were back in the car. "And now we have someone who has a motive to stitch up Danny Kellog."

"A bit of a stretch, surely?" Verity said. "Still holding a grudge for a schoolboy fight twenty-five years ago?"

"If Josie's got it right—and I bet she has—this was a young fellow who fancied himself as the big man being publicly beaten in front of everyone. In southern Italy centuries-long feuds have started over less. I'm sure," she added, "that the Welsh were never so foolish."

"You underestimate us, ma'am. We can do feuds. The great Welsh historian Sir John Wynne of Gwydir said that in the six-teenth century if squires in North Wales wanted a peaceful life they'd best move abroad, since life at home presented them with no alternative but to kill or be killed by their relatives!"

"I knew there had to be a reason why we get on so well."

"Thank you, ma'am. Now that I think about it, what Josie

says about Shpend at school does seem more or less to fit with Bert Tern's impression of him when he was a few years older. A nasty piece of work, and he fancied himself. Not that Bert is likely to be the best witness in the world as to character."

Cecilia shrugged. "Oh, I don't know. Bert was bent but that doesn't mean he was stupid. He had some pretty good results when he was young. That's what's so sad."

"Even so," Verity said, "and whatever may have happened way back when the Kellogs and the Morinas were all at school in Bermondsey, what we *still* don't have is a shred of evidence that Shpend Morina's ever been *near* Edgestow, let alone amusing himself trying to stitch up Danny Kellog for killing Sister Barbara and stealing a painting."

"Exactly," Cecilia said. "We need to talk to him."

"We need to *find* him," Verity said.

THIRTY-ONE

Edgestow. Wednesday, 14th November.

It is standard British humor — and in general by no means ill-intentioned — to refer to police as "the Plod." But the fact is, vital evidence in a case is often uncovered not by brilliant detective instinct or intuition but by painstaking, methodical examination of hundreds — sometimes even thousands — of possible sources of information: in other words, by plodding, which in matters such as this is perhaps just another word for tenacity. And it was so on this occasion. Verity Jones got the "shred of evidence" about Shpend Morina's presence in Edgestow that she wanted, and sooner than she might have expected. And it all came about through plodding.

For the second time that week everyone living in the road where the Kellogs lived and in the roads adjoining received a visit from the police: and this time they were shown a photograph of Shpend Morina.

Had they had seen him?

And one person, a young woman, thought that she had. She went so far (unprompted) as to say that the man in the photograph was "sitting in a car and seemed to be staring at Mr. and Mrs. Kellog's house." That had been in the afternoon of Guy Fawkes. She remembered what day it was, because she'd been carrying home the stuff she'd bought at the supermarket for a special tea and then they were all going out later to see the fireworks.

What kind of car?

She couldn't be sure. Fairly large, it was. Dark colored, probably darkish red, she thought. Not *very* dark, but not scarlet.

Any idea of the make?

Not a clue. But it looked like a nice car.

"Right," the constable said, and wrote it all down.

Shpend's photograph was also shown in the local shops, the Post Office, and nearby pubs, including The Great Western. Mostly the results were negative, as of course they always are — mostly.

But then the observant Jennifer Pettigrew at The Great Western came up trumps.

She was *sure* she remembered him, she told the constable. He was a quiet man with a beard who drank pints of draft bitter. He'd been in two or three times over the weekend.

She hadn't liked him much.

Why not?

Well, he was civil enough. But she'd thought him a bit creepy. No, she couldn't really say why.

The last time she saw him in the bar — she was pretty sure of this — was on Guy Fawkes' night. He was with another man. She didn't think he'd been in since.

THIRTY-TWO

Edgestow. Later the same day.

A car that was "darkish red."

This was interesting. Sister Chiara had seen a dark red car parked for a long time on the road past the abbey just before the break-in. And the observant sister had known what kind of car it was.

The constable was duly sent round again to the young woman who lived in the same road as the Kellogs, this time with several photographs of dark red cars, among them a Mercedes Benz C Class.

She picked the Mercedes at once.

Jennifer Pettigrew said she'd seen Shpend and another man together in The Great Western.

That, too, was interesting. Even promising.

Cecilia and Verity went round to see her and check the details.

They began, however, by talking to her about Danny Kellog's alibi.

"Mr. Kellog came in about a quarter past ten," Jennifer said. "He said he'd just have a pint and then he'd have to be off home to Josie — that's Mrs. Kellog."

Cecilia nodded.

"Well then about a quarter to eleven he got a call on his mobile. He said it was Mrs. Kellog saying she was coming down here with their mates that live down the road in their car, and they could make an evening of it."

"In their mates' car?"

"Yes. Then she could drive herself and Mr. Kellog home in *their* car because she doesn't drink—leastways, not more than a glass, and then she makes it last all night! So Mr. Kellog said oh good, that meant he could have another pint. She and their friends—Mr. and Mrs. Levovitch and Mr. and Mrs. Nichol—showed up about eleven and they were here pretty well till we closed, which that night was one-thirty. Because of Guy Fawkes."

"Where did they sit, Jennifer?"

"Over there in the corner. Handy for the bar, as Mr. Kellog always says!"

"So you had a good view of them? And you don't think Mr. Kellog ever left the party?"

"Not for more than five minutes, top weight. I mean, I think he went to the loo a couple of times. That was all. I think Dad will say the same. Mr. Kellog *is* rather noticeable, ma'am! So is Mrs. Kellog, come to that!"

Cecilia smiled and nodded. They'd already talked with Jim Pettigrew, who had indeed said the same as his daughter.

She looked at Verity.

It would take at least fifteen minutes to drive to the abbey, and then at the least ten minutes to get over the wall, commit a murder, and then return—assuming he'd been lucky and virtually found Sister Barbara waiting for him—and then at least another fifteen minutes to get back to The Great Western. What was more, he would have been obliged to leave the bar and re-enter it by the main entrance. They'd checked the toilets earlier to see if someone might have pretended to spend time in them, while in fact leaving and returning by a window. But the only windows in the toilets were high up and small. A cat might have left and returned that way, but the notion that a man of Danny Kellog's build had done it was absurd.

"Not even Houdini," Cecilia said with a sigh. "That didn't happen."

Of course they'd checked earlier with Levovitches and the Nicholses, who said Danny Kellog had been with them the whole time. Friends who are drinking and enjoying themselves can sometimes not notice passing minutes during which someone is absent—but *forty* minutes (at least)? Hardly.

Cecilia again produced the photograph of Shpend Morina.

"Jennifer, you say that you saw this man on Guy Fawkes night?"

"Yes, ma'am. I told the constable."

"You didn't mention him in the list you gave us of those who were here between 11:00 and 1:30. Did seeing the photograph jog your memory?"

Or was she saying she'd seen him because she rather enjoyed being a key witness and thought that was what the police wanted her to have seen? Cecilia liked Jennifer, but she'd liked witnesses before who turned out to be too fond of being witnesses.

Jennifer's reply, however, was straightforward and made sense.

"No ma'am. I didn't mention him earlier because he wasn't here then, not between 11:00 and 1:30, the times you were asking about. He came in with another man some time after ten, just a few minutes after Mr. Kellog, as I remember, and they sat in the booth where you like to sit. He came up to the bar and ordered a pint of bitter for himself and a Perrier for the man with him. But then they left at about twenty to eleven—just as we started to get busy. I remember because he—that's the man in the photograph—had just ordered another round and gone back with it to where they were sitting. So I thought they'd stay a bit longer. But then he must have just poured it down his throat, because the pair of them got up the next minute and left."

"What did the other man look like, Jennifer? The man he was with? What do you remember?"

"Well, he was sort of middling height—a bit smaller than the man with the beard. And sort of middling build. And the way he moved, I'd say he wasn't old. I mean, he wasn't *old* old. And he was wearing a windcheater, with the hood up."

"Did you get to see his face?"

"No, ma'am, I never did. When they came in he had his hood up like I said and he went straight into the booth and you can't see in there from here."

"And you didn't get a glimpse of his face even when he left?"

"No, I didn't. I mean, it wasn't like I paid a lot of attention and I'm not saying he was trying to hide his face, but if he had been he couldn't have done a better job of it, now I come to think about it."

Cecilia smiled.

"All right," she said. "Now, I want to be quite sure about this, Jennifer. These men—the man in this photograph and the other man—came into the bar here soon after Mr. Kellog came in?"

"Yes, ma'am."

"So they might have heard Mr. Kellog saying he was going to leave the pub and go home after just one pint?"

Jennifer laughed.

"I should think the whole pub heard, ma'am. I mean, I do like Mr. Kellog. In fact I like them both. Mrs. Kellog always makes us laugh. But neither of them is exactly quiet!"

"So then they—the men in the booth—even though they'd just got a fresh round of drinks and must have drunk them in a hurry, got up and left?"

"Yes."

"So do you think they'd have heard Mr. Kellog say he'd

changed his mind and was going to stay here after all? Would they have heard about the phone call from Mrs. Kellog saying she was coming down?"

"No, ma'am. They wouldn't."

"You seem very sure of that, Jennifer. Why wouldn't they have heard?"

"I am sure. I remember, because I was just coming back from collecting the empty glasses — including the ones from the booth where they'd been — when I heard Mr. Kellog telling Dad that Mrs. Kellog was coming here with their friends, and so he'd changed his mind about going home straight away."

Cecilia exchanged a glance with Verity, and nodded. It sounded convincing.

"Thank you, Jennifer. You've been very helpful."

"Do you think you can catch whoever it was murdered Sister Barbara now? Was it those men?"

"We would like to talk to them. We think perhaps they can help us in our inquiries."

"Jennifer," Verity said, "that sand butt for cigarette ends on the way in, by the main door. Was it there on Guy Fawkes night?"

"Oh, yes, ma'am," Jennifer said. "It's always there. There's no smoking in the bar now, you see, not since the Health Act. So people have to put out their cigarettes and things before they come in."

"If you don't mind," Verity said, "I'm just going to nick a little bit of your sand when we leave. It could be important. I assume it *is* the same sand that was in the butt on Guy Fawkes night."

"Yes, ma'am. One of us just clears the cigarette ends out every day, and then we top the barrel up with some fresh sand from the pile round the back. But it's been the same pile of sand for months. Dad bought it ages ago."

Well spotted, Verity!

THIRTY-THREE

Edgestow. The car park of The Great Western,
a few minutes later.

Outside in the car park it was drizzling.

But Cecilia was well content to turn her collar up and wait while Verity collected her specimen of sand from the butt by the door and put it into an evidence bag.

They got back into the car.

"I think," Cecilia said cautiously, "that we may have the beginning of a scenario."

"Try it," Verity said.

"You be Shpend Morina."

"All right."

"You know who and where the hated Ariana is, who betrayed you all."

"How do I know that?"

"Because Granddad told the whole family, and he did that because even though she'd changed her name she was still family and must be protected. That's more or less what his sons said."

"All right."

"But you're the new generation and you think granddad was a sentimental old fool and anyway he's dead now and six feet under. So you've come to Edgestow to pay your cousin out for what she did and for getting you twenty years in the slammer."

"Okay. I suppose I might have decided to do that."

"And we've got one tiny bit of evidence suggesting that you did. Remember when we talked to Armend Morina, he *evaded* rather than denying the suggestion that a member of the family had killed Ariana? And if it *was* a family member then surely Shpend, the only one of the men out of jail, would be the obvious candidate."

"What about the women? One of those elusive ladies we haven't found yet? This is the twenty-first century, as I keep reminding you, ma'am. We can do murder!"

"I rather think we always could," Cecilia said. "And I haven't forgotten about the women. Checking on their whereabouts is already on Joseph's to-do list. If we draw a blank on Shpend, that's where I'll go next. But for the moment, let's keep trying with Shpend."

"All right. I'm Shpend and I've come to Edgestow to pay out my niece for what she did."

"Cousin."

"Right, cousin."

"So—you plan it for Guy Fawkes night, which seems a suitable evening for blowing up a nasty traitor. And there'll be fireworks and crowds and general confusion."

"Whoa, ma'am! How do I know that before I get here? Edgestow's events aren't exactly published in the Court Circular."

"Point taken … Wait a minute, let's back up. You *didn't* know before you got here. You just came here because you knew it was where Ariana was, because grandfather Jakov had told you all, and you were out to get her. But then of course you had to spy out the land for a day or two—to work out how you were going to do it."

"That's better. Jennifer in The Great Western said she'd seen me around for a day or so."

"So you watch the sisters for a day or two — remember Tom Foss said that the wall to the abbey had been climbed several times."

"Probably three times, I think it was. And Chiara said there'd been a car like mine parked outside the abbey the day before I did the deed. So it looks as if I'd done some daylight watching, too."

"Right — and while you're here you also learn what's going on in the town, and *then* decide to do it on Guy Fawkes night. By now you've got some idea of the sisters' routine, and Sister Barbara's — that's Ariana's to you — habit of walking alone before she turns in, and that's going to give you the perfect opportunity."

"All right. That might pass."

"And somehow — to be honest I've no idea how — you also know about the sisters' painting. A painting that could make you a lot of money."

"That could be to do with the chap I'm with on Guy Fawkes night. And we know of at least two people who knew about that painting — Abrahams and Shale — so I suppose it could even be one of them that I've linked up with. Jennifer's description could fit either of them."

"It could also fit half the population of the United Kingdom. But still, you're right. It could be one of them."

Verity grinned. "Or someone else!"

"Then while you and your mate are waiting in the pub until it's time to start, you spot Danny Kellog, the boy who humiliated you at school. You can't believe your luck! You can work things so as both to kill the traitor Ariana *and* frame that sanctimonious prig who beat you up at school!"

"No."

"No?"

"It's too pat. I mean, I can swallow 'I can't believe my luck' and so on. But I surely spotted Kellog earlier: though probably it *was* in The Great Western. He's a regular, and as the admirable and observant Jennifer points out, he's rather noticeable. And if I spotted him earlier that gave me time to work all this out."

"All right. What if—"

"Hang on! I think I can do this. I spotted Kellog and recognized him earlier in the day or even the previous day. And then I followed him—that's how I found out where he lives. And that's when I'm seen sitting in my dark red Mercedes C Class looking at the house. Don't you wish you could afford a dark red Mercedes C Class, ma'am?"

"Stick to the point Verity. But yes, there you are, tailing him in your dark red Merc. Then what?"

"I'm not sure how long I go on tailing him, but eventually I follow him to The Great Western, or *back* to The Great Western, if that's where I saw him first. And there, while I'm still in my car in the car park, maybe waiting for my pal to turn up—remember they were in separate cars, according to Foss and Gibbins—I see him stuff his cigar into the sand butt. And I realize what a great piece of evidence that would be if it were near the murder scene that we're going to create."

"Even better. I like it."

"So I pick up the stub and then when my pal arrives we go into the pub and we hear Danny shooting his mouth off about how he's going to go home after just one pint—which means if we go and do the deed now, Danny will have very little alibi to speak of. Just his wife, who'd be bound to speak up for him."

"So you drink up and leave at once—thereby missing the vital change in Danny's plans!"

"Actually," Verity said, "maybe I don't drink up. Not if I'm the one who's just ordered the pint. Do you remember the day after Guy Fawkes, the plant by our booth that stank of beer?"

"I do! He could have poured it in there. That makes sense."

"Anyway," Verity said, "we leave, thereby missing the change in Danny's plans. We murder Sister Barbara and steal the painting, leave the incriminating cigar near the wall, and come back to Edgestow. Then one of us creeps back to Danny's house later that night and buries the incriminating shoes and tracksuit in his garden."

"Apropos the tracksuit, you might even have taken the trouble to snag it on purpose the last time you went over the wall — just to make sure there was a connection."

"I might have done just that."

The two sat looking at each other.

"Do you think anything like that might actually be what happened?" Cecilia said.

"I don't know. I suppose it could. There's still a colossal gap in it, though."

"Who on earth *was* the other one? And what's his connection with Shpend?"

Verity nodded.

"Obviously," she said, "Abrahams and Shale are still in the frame. But they were in it anyway. And plenty of other people could have noticed there was a valuable painting in the abbey. Shale has his staff. I bet Abrahams has someone to do his letters. Any of them could have talked to their spouse or their lover or their boyfriend. Once you start thinking about it, the possibilities are legion."

Cecilia nodded.

"And," she said, "although we now have sightings suggesting that Shpend's been in Edgestow, visiting Edgestow isn't in itself a crime, and we don't have a *thing* connecting him with the actual crime scene. As you've pointed out, we don't even know where he is."

"Alas, true!"

"All right, those are the negatives. But now let's be positive. If Shpend Morina *was* in Edgestow for those few days — and for the moment I'm proceeding on the hypothesis that our witnesses got it right—then he must have stayed somewhere. He could have camped out or he could have found digs. My guess is digs: I don't see him as the camping sort. But we need to check everything: every house that might take in lodgers, every farmer round here who might let someone camp in a field. House to house: we need to find out where he's stayed. And if we're going to get on with it, it'll take more officers than we've got. Edgestow isn't all that big, but it isn't all that small, either. Exeter will have to help. I'll call Davies. And you talk to Sergeant Wyatt about starting as many of our own people on it as are available right away."

"Understood, ma'am."

"Also we need forensics to look at your cigar stub—and while we're on the subject of forensics I'd like to know when we can expect anything from them about the tracksuit and the trainers."

"On it, ma'am!" Verity paused, then added, "And at least now we've got one thing we didn't have before."

"What's that?"

"A real suspect."

"The trouble is, we really need two suspects."

"One out of two is a start!"

"That's true. And incidentally, no, I don't wish I could afford a Mercedes C class, even if it was dark red. What I mean is, if I could afford it, that wouldn't be what I'd buy. I'd buy a bright red Alfa Romeo Giulietta."

"Of course you'd want an Italian car. That's only patriotic. I should have thought of that."

"It's nothing to do with patriotism. It's a known fact—a truth universally acknowledged—that Italian cars are the best. Everyone who knows anything about anything knows that."

"Yes, ma'am."

THIRTY-FOUR

Edgestow. Thursday, 15th November.

Once again, plodding police work produced a result.

First in was forensics. Tom Foss telephoned Cecilia.

"Here's what we've got. First the bad news — there's nothing in the tracksuit or the shoes to show they were ever handled by the chap whose DNA we found on the cigar, Kellog. There are traces of earth on them which I assume came from his garden — though I haven't checked that against a specimen — but since you found them there that wouldn't tell you anything you didn't know already."

"Right."

"Apropos the cigar that *did* have Kellog's saliva on it, the sand on it is indeed a perfect match for the specimen of sand that you gave me — from the butt outside The Great Western, wasn't it? Obviously, that's not the only example of that kind of sand in the world, but the match would certainly fit with its having been stubbed out in that."

"All right."

"Now, back to the tracksuit and trainers. Interestingly enough, both of them — and I mean the trainers too — have evidently been recently washed. I'd say in a washing machine. That was before they were buried, of course. Which makes me think someone was trying to remove DNA evidence. It's amazing to me how many people think that will work. Of course it will remove some kinds of evidence—but not anything solid. Which brings me to the good news."

"That will be nice."

"First, the tracksuit is definitely the one in which someone climbed over the wall at the abbey. You remember we found threads on the wall?"

"I remember."

"Well the snag on the tracksuit is obvious, and the match to the threads perfect."

"Right. Good."

"But what I think is really important is that we found a human hair in one of the seams in the tracksuit. I guess it would have caught there when it was pulled over someone's head."

"And?"

Tom Foss was a good chap, but he did like to draw things out.

"And," he continued, "we have a match for the DNA."

"And?"

"Well, as I said, it's not Kellog."

"So you did."

For God's sake man!

"But it *is* on the data base. A fellow called Shpend Morina—"

"Cheers!" Cecilia said.

"Oh, is that good? I thought you were looking at the cigar man."

"I was for a bit. But that's changed. Sorry—I should have kept you in the loop. Shpend Morina is my prime suspect now. And you chaps have just pretty well linked him to the crime scene. Which is brilliant."

"Oh! Well good! And no need to apologize—actually, I always find it more convincing when I find something that I'm not actually looking for, if you see what I mean."

"I do see what you mean. And so do I—find it more convincing, I mean. Thank you, Tom. You are all utterly brilliant."

The next piece of slow work to produce a result was the inquiry as to where Shpend Morina might have stayed during his visit to Edgestow. Four of Cecilia's own constables, supplemented by six more from Exeter, had shown his photograph and inquired after him at every house in every street in Edgestow and the nearby village of St. Anne's, as well as at surrounding farms. Finally, at the end of a long day, they came to Gloucester Terrace, the road where Cecilia herself was living. And there at last a Mrs. Bailey, who lived only six houses down from Mrs. Abney and, like her, took in paying guests, recognized the man in the photograph. He had stayed with her for three nights.

"I may have walked past him in the street!" Cecilia said. "Isn't it odd how when you're trying to find something, it invariably turns out to be in the last place you look?"

"Surely that's because when you find it you stop looking?" Verity said.

Cecilia looked at her for a moment in silence.

"Well," she said, "let's go and see Mrs. Bailey, shall we?"

Mrs. Bailey did indeed remember the man in the photograph, although not by that name.

"That's right, that's Mr. Blake," she said, looking at the photograph Cecilia showed her. "Like I said to your constable, he was here for three nights. He came on Saturday. A bit of a weirdo, I thought."

Cecilia made her "mother-confessor" noise and waited.

"I don't mean he caused any problem or anything. He was all right that way, paid in advance with cash for his three nights, all fine. But he come in very late every night—I give them a key, of course, I prefer not to be bothered—and on his last night,

Tuesday, after Guy Fawkes, well, Wednesday morning, really, he come in about half past twelve and then he was running the washing machine and the dryer in the utility room. God knows what he was washing at that time of night!"

Cecilia exchanged a glance with Verity.

"Anyway," Mrs. Bailey continued, "then he went to bed. But he was up again about five and he left straightaway, drove off in the dark. Didn't wait for his breakfast or to say cheerio or anything. Of course he'd paid and all that, so he was free to do what he liked, but as I say, a bit of a weirdo."

Cecilia nodded.

"I take it he — Mr. Blake — had a car, Mrs. Bailey?"

"Oh yes. He come in it and drove off in it, like I said."

"Did you notice what kind of car?"

"I'm afraid not. They all look the same to me. But it was quite posh."

"DS Jones?"

Verity produced several photographs of cars, one of which was a dark red Mercedes-Benz C Class C180. Mrs. Bailey looked at them for a moment, frowned, and finally picked the Mercedes.

"I think that was it. It looked like that."

"Did he give you any idea where he might be going?" Verity asked.

Mrs. Bailey shook her head.

"Not that I recall. I mean, not that we talked much. I think once at breakfast he said something about getting back to the smoke."

Cecilia nodded.

"That sounds to me like something a Londoner would say."

"So let me just go through this," Chief Superintendent Davies said when Cecilia phoned him and communicated the latest. "You've now got evidence virtually tying Shpend Morina to the crime scene. He's got a probable motive, and he's got a criminal record that includes violence. Is that right?"

"I think so sir."

"Well that's quite enough to bring him in for questioning. Since it looks as though he's left Edgestow, we'll need to have a wide net out for him. Given the possibility he was going back to London, I'll get the Met onto it. But I'll also get an APW out. We don't want him skipping the country. We can also check with vehicle registrations and see have they have a car for Shpend. Leave all that to us, Cavaliere. You and your team have done well. Tell them that from me. And I'll keep you posted."

"Thank you sir."

"I called Tom Foss, by the way," Cecilia said to Verity half an hour or so later, "and he says the tire marks of one of those two cars that were parked by the abbey on the night of the murder — the one that was driven by the Nike LeBron Xs — were Pirelli P4s, which means they *could* have been made by a Mercedes C class."

"Ah, but could it have been a dark red one?"

"Idiot!"

"Anyway," Verity said, "I've got some news for you. Chief Superintendent Davies's office phoned while you were talking to Foss. They've contacted the Ministry of Transport database for vehicle registrations, and there's a result! A 2011 Mercedes-Benz C Class Coupe C280 is registered as belonging to one Shpend Morina."

"Excellent."

"Unfortunately, the address they have is the same as the Met had — in other words, it's useless. The good news is, we now have a registration number. They've notified the Met, and ANPR will be watching for it, so unless he's changed the plates, if Shpend drives that car again anywhere in the UK, sooner or later we'll get him."

Cecilia nodded. Automatic Number Plate Recognition cameras, established in Britain since 2006 and linked to the Police National Computer, were an invaluable way of keeping track of vehicles the police were interested in.

"Good. Well let's hope he hasn't changed them."

"He'd probably want to keep his own car legit. Nobody wants to drive for long on false plates, and he has no reason yet even to think we're on to him."

Cecilia nodded.

"I hope you're right. I think you may be. In which case, for the moment we should probably just do what we're best at."

"What's that, ma'am?"

"Wait."

THIRTY-FIVE

Deptford Police Station, London. The same evening.

The national police network duly circulated photographs of Shpend Morina, details of his car, and requests for information about his whereabouts.

As a result of which ANPR came up almost at once with a sighting of the Mercedes near Southwark Bridge early that afternoon — welcome confirmation that Shpend was back in South London — and then, at about eight o'clock on the Friday evening, Detective Inspector Bill Sanders, based at Deptford Police Station in Amersham Vale, was handed fresh records of the car being identified in Grange Road: twice that day.

He stood, thinking.

Grange Road ... Grange Road ... wait a minute, that was near Grove Road, and that was where Shpend Morina's former girlfriend lived, wasn't it? — the one he used to like to beat up? What was her name? Denise ... Denise something. Something stupid. Denise Lemon. That was it. Lemon by name and a lemon by nature. Ten to one he was shacked up with her again.

"Well and good," he said to himself. "If that's the case, we'll have him."

He called for back up — Shpend Morina was inclined to be violent — and was told it was on its way. He then turned to two uniformed constables — one man, one woman — who'd just come on duty and looked as if they thought they might begin with a cup of tea.

"Jarvis, Bridges, you're with me!"

PCs Jarvis and Bridges exchanged a glance.

"So much for that cup of tea," Jarvis muttered.

"Cup of tea? Where's your sense of glory?" Sanders said, and did not stay for an answer.

The flat was on the fifth floor of a pleasant, reasonably respectable block.

They rang the doorbell and banged on the door.

From within came sounds of movement and a radio. But the door did not open.

Bill Sanders banged again.

"Come on, Denise!" he said. "Police! Open up!"

"Have you got a search warrant?"

Bill raised his eyes to heaven. Everyone watched too much TV crime these days.

"Pack it in, Denise!" he shouted back. "I don't need a warrant if I'm going to arrest someone. Now are you going to open up or shall we break the door down?"

"Let me get some clothes on then!" came from the other side of the door. "I was just going to have a bath."

Bill pointed to the gap under the door.

"What can you see?" he said to Constable Jarvis, who got down on his knees and peered.

"Bare feet with painted toenails jumping about!"

DI Sanders was a decent man.

"You've got thirty seconds," he shouted, "so get on with it!"

A few more seconds passed and the door opened to reveal a tousled young woman in a blue dressing gown. She had one bruised eye — the bruise looked to be a couple of days old — and a cut, which looked fresh, over the other eye.

"As you know very well, Denise, I'm Detective Inspector Sanders of the Metropolitan police," Sanders said, showing his warrant card. "And we're looking for your old pal Shpend Morina. Is he here?"

"He's gone away," she said.

"Then you'll be happy to invite us in, won't you, Denise? Thank you!"

The girl looked anxious but made no objection as he brushed past her.

"That cut over your eye looks nasty, miss. How did you get that?" Constable Bridges asked.

"I bumped into the fridge door."

"Really! Will you let me look at it?"

Bill Sanders meanwhile had gone into the bedroom, followed by Jarvis.

The window was open. The bed was unmade.

Sanders felt the bedclothes. They were warm on both sides of the bed.

"He was here," he said. "The bugger's scarpered. Where's he gone?"

"He's gone down the fire escape," Jarvis said from the window.

"Don't be bloody ridiculous. There *is* no fire escape."

"There is, sir. I'm after him!" Jarvis said, and went out of the window.

Sanders leaped to the window.

"Jesus Christ, so there is!" He pulled out his mobile. "Backup! Where are you?"

"Grange Road, sir."

"Morina's done a runner down a back fire escape. He'll be in Grove Mews. But there's only one way out of that. Cut him off at the corner, will you?"

In the hallway PC Bridges was applying a plaster to Denise Lemon's cut.

"How long has that fire escape been there?" Sanders asked.

"Couple of months," Denise said. "New regulations. Health and safety! Council said we were a fire hazard."

"Damn!" he said. "How the hell was I supposed to know that?" — and charged out through the front door.

Shpend Morina was breathing hard as he jumped from the fire escape and ran down Grove Mews. He got to the corner and stopped. To his left he could see the flashing lights of a police car as it turned into Gorham Road. So that direction was blocked. Well, that was fine. Denise's lockup was in Yard Lane to his right. If he could just get to the corner, he'd be there in minutes, and in the Mercedes minutes later. He fingered the keys in his pocket. He reckoned he'd back the Mercedes against anything the police were likely to have. He just had to get to it. He began to walk towards the corner, steeling himself to move slowly, to stay calm, above all not to draw attention to himself by running.

If only those damned streetlights weren't so bright.

From the opposite end of the road came the soft but powerful sound of another engine. Now what? He stopped. A big motorcycle with twin headlights was coming towards him, its rider a dim shadow behind the glare. He screwed up his eyes, dazzled, but then the beams turned away from him as the motorcycle pulled onto his side of the road and stopped, about four meters away, its engine running quietly, silky smooth and powerful. Now he could see it properly: a rider and a pillion passenger, both small and slim, in dark, shining leathers and full-face helmets.

The rider turned toward him.

"Shpend Morina, I think."

The voice was light and sounded educated.

"Who wants to know?"

"We do," the rider said. "And what luck! We were ready to wait around for you for hours if we had to."

"And who are you?"

"Nemesis," the figure on the pillion said, speaking for the first time, and raised its right hand. He found himself staring down the barrel of a Glock 42 semi automatic pistol, now pointed directly at him.

As Bill Sanders ran up Grove Road towards the corner, he heard the sound of a motor, then voices.

He pounded the last few meters.

Now he was near enough to hear words.

"Your sister Ariana was a princess — you weren't fit to lick her boots. Grandfather knew that. This is for disrespecting him."

A shot, followed by a scream of pain.

"And this for Ariana."

Three more shots, in rapid succession.

PC George Collins, driving down Gorham Road towards Grove Mews, saw it all.

"Christ," he muttered as the man by the wall went down, "that's done for him or I'm a Dutchman."

As they approached, the motorcycle pulled out from the curbside, crossed in front of them, and passed by them on their right, accelerating rapidly. He could see it in his mirror as it came up to the T-junction at the far end on the street, turned left into Grange Road, and disappeared from his sight.

He brought the car to a halt and he and his partner Bill Bryant got out. Shpend Morina lay on the paving stones, blood seeping from his chest and his crotch in a widening pool.

PC Jarvis ran out from Grove Mews. Seconds later DI Sanders emerged from Grove Road.

Both pulled up short and surveyed the scene.

"Jesus Christ," Sanders said, "what a bloody mess!"

He knelt and felt Morina's neck.

He looked up, and shook his head.

"Nothing. He's gone. Call an ambulance."

"Yes, sir," Collins said.

Sanders got to his feet, then looked down at the body again.

"Too clever for his own good, that one," he said. "If he'd let us collar him he'd still be alive."

Meanwhile Collins had got through on his mobile.

"Oh don't worry, we'll still be here," he said to whoever was dispatching that night, "and the patient certainly isn't going anywhere."

He switched off the phone.

"There's an ambulance on its way."

He looked dubiously along the road, then back at DI Sanders.

"I'm sorry sir, I wasn't sure what to do just now. Should I have gone after them?"

Sanders shook his head.

"They'd have been in the next borough before you got the car turned round."

"They came from the other end of the street, sir."

Sanders nodded.

"I dare say they did. And they knew exactly what they were doing."

"How'd they know he'd be here?"

"They knew where he was living," Sanders said, "and I imagine they were prepared to wait around for as long as it took."

He gave Collins a wan smile.

"In other words," he said, "and in case you've never seen one before, *that*, Constable Collins, was a professional hit. You can be quite sure that when ballistics examine the bullets they'll find they have nothing whatever in the databases on the weapon that fired them, and no one will find anything anywhere that will give so much as a clue as to who did it. I don't suppose you got a sight of the shooters?"

"Only leathers and helmets, sir. I'm not even sure if they were men or women. The motorcycle was some kind of super-bike. I think maybe a Ducati? — but I couldn't see the plates."

"They'll be false anyway. And they've probably changed them already."

THIRTY-SIX

Heavitree Police Station. Mid-morning, Saturday, 17th November.

Cecilia laid down the report and looked up at Glyn Davies.
"So," she said, "taking one consideration with another, and not to put too fine a point on it, the Metropolitan police just screwed up a perfectly straightforward arrest. And as a result they now have an entirely new murder inquiry on their hands."

"I suppose they were a bit unlucky," Davies said. "The fire escape had only been there for two months and no one knew about it. And even then I dare say they'd still have got him if it hadn't been for a pair of thoroughly professional hit men turning up out of the blue."

"With the greatest respect, sir — "

"Whenever you say that, Cavaliere, I know I'm in trouble."

"*With* the greatest respect, sir," Cecilia said, "I can hear exactly what you'd be saying if this was one of us. Two months is quite a long time! We should have checked before we went charging in! Time spent on reconnaissance is never wasted!"

Davies gave a faint smile.

"Well," he said, "I dare say you have a point."

He looked back at the file copy on his computer screen.

"On the bright side," he said, "it looks as if we can draw two red lines under the murder part of our own inquiry. You see what the report says about that."

The Met had found leather gloves in the flat where Shpend had been living. London and Exeter's forensics between them had already confirmed that they were the gloves used to strangle Sister Barbara. They reeked of Shpend's sweat and prints, and no one else's. In other words, they were his gloves, and he was the only one who had worn them. So he must be the one who committed the murder. Beyond all reasonable doubt! Even the rigorists and agnostics of the Crown Prosecution Service would surely have conceded that.

By way of gilt upon the gingerbread, they had also found Shpend's Mercedes in Denise Lemon's lockup. Everything, down to a slight irregularity in the tread of one of its Pirelli P4s, confirmed that it was one of the two cars that had parked in the road alongside St. Boniface Abbey on the night of the murder.

So surely — case solved?

Quod erat demonstrandum.

"That's all very well," Cecilia said. "But if only we actually had Shpend Morina in custody instead of on his back in the morgue, there's every reason to think he'd *also* know something about the painting and where that's gone. I don't suppose the woman he was with has anything useful to say?"

"I gather she's one of those rather sad people who fancies men who knock her about. The Met doesn't think she knows anything at all."

Cecilia nodded, but being, it seemed, in an unforgiving mood today, could not resist a final scratch, "As for the Met not being prepared for professional hit, they should have been. We'd warned them about Armend's threats. They made a mess of the whole thing."

"Ah, well now there's a funny thing," Davies said. "I've been talking to them about that. Of course after what happened last night they questioned Armend Morina and the rest of the family members — in Belmarsh this morning, actually. But *they* deny all knowledge of it, or who was behind it."

"So there's a surprise! I mean they would, wouldn't they?"

"There's more to it than that. The man I talked to was one of the officers who did the interviewing — a Detective Superintendent David Landon. He's a good man. *He* wouldn't have screwed up your arrest! Anyway, he tells me it wasn't just that the Morinas denied doing it. Armend in particular made no bones about the fact he'd *intended* to take out a contract on Shpend. Even said he'd more or less told you he'd do it, even if it was his own son."

Cecilia nodded.

"He did say that, more or less in those words."

"But Armend pointed out this morning there was no way he'd had time to arrange it yet. And he seemed, if anything, not so much anxious to make us believe it wasn't him, or even annoyed about what had happened, as amused that someone else had beaten him to it.'

"*Amused*? This was his son, for God's sake."

"Armend is a hard man. Ariana was his niece, and she was under Jakov Morina's protection — which was to say, the family's protection. So Shpend had broken the rules. He'd disrespected his grandfather's wishes and he'd dishonored the family. And apparently those breaches of protocol counted for more *against* him than being Armend's son counted *for* him. Don't ask me to explain it. Anyway, Armend seemed to think that family honor was now satisfied. Whether he actually knows who did it is another question. Landon thought he had a pretty good idea. But if so he certainly wasn't telling."

Cecilia nodded.

"I must say, I'd quite like to have another go at Armend Morina on that."

Davies shook his head.

"Not your case, Cavaliere."

He looked back at the report.

"Just between ourselves, there's one thing I find odd about this," he said.

Cecilia looked at him.

"The bullets they took out of Shpend Morina! They were .380s. In a professional hit I'd have expected the killers to use something heavier—something with more obvious stopping power. That's all. Whoever fired the shots obviously knew exactly what he was doing. They were perfectly placed. So I suppose we just have a killer who likes a light weapon. But I was surprised."

Cecilia nodded.

"Actually, sir, there's one thing that *I* find odd."

"Which is?"

"It's the part reported by DI Sanders." She peered at the report again. "Yes, that's it. He says he heard the killer say, 'Your sister Ariana was worth ten of you'—or something like that."

"That's right."

"Well, Ariana wasn't his sister, was she? She was his cousin."

"Maybe Sanders misheard. There was a lot going on."

"I don't see how you could mishear 'cousin' as 'sister.'"

Davies nodded.

"Maybe they just made a mistake," he said. "If they were professional killers, they'd been hired to do a job, hadn't they? Not to memorize the family tree!"

THIRTY-SEVEN

Exeter. St. Mary's Rectory. Just before noon, the same day.

Before driving back to Edgestow, Cecilia went home to the rectory for an early light lunch with Michael and Rachel.

Michael boiled eggs for all of them, and made toast, including soldiers for Rachel. Being in the kitchen with her husband and daughter, together with Figaro and Felix and Marlene, calmed Cecilia considerably.

But still she had to give some vent to her frustrations.

"We'd have had him," she said to Michael. "It's absolutely certain he was our man. He'd have cracked in an interview sure as eggs, and then we'd not only have had him, we'd have had something on where our Madonna's gone. As it is, some idiot in the Met's gone and messed up a perfectly straightforward arrest and as far as the painting's concerned we're back to square one. It's absolutely maddening."

"Oh, Mama! Che disastro!" Rachel said.

Cecilia turned her attention to her daughter, who was referring, however, not to the failures of the Metropolitan Police but to the fact that in the process of carefully dipping her soldier into her egg she had tipped over the beaker that held her orange juice.

Fortunately the beaker was plastic, and she had already drunk most of the juice.

"Tutt'a posto, tesoro," Cecilia said gently. "Stai calma!"

She moved the beaker to a safer place, and mopped up the few drops of orange juice with a napkin.

"So what have you chaps been up to today while I've been protecting freedom and democracy?" she asked Michael.

"We've had a *very* interesting time, haven't we sweetheart?" he said.

Rachel nodded vigorously, her mouth now full of egg and toast, while Figaro thumped his tail.

"Lisa and Lucretia are coming in this afternoon to clean the house, because they couldn't come yesterday," Michael said. "So of course Rachel and I have had to spend most of the morning tidying up first, so that the place will be fit for them to come into! You've no idea what a pickle it was in."

Cecilia chuckled.

"I bet I have," she said. "Anyway, it sounds as if you've both had a more useful morning than I have. And at the end of the day the house will be shining and perfect!"

"Right," Michael said. "Or at least," he added, "it will be for about five minutes."

"Daddy, did the bad people win?" Rachel asked when her mother had departed for Edgestow and she and Michael were putting plates and spoons and eggcups into the dishwasher. "Mummy didn't seem happy today."

"Well, sweetheart, it's a bit more complicated than that. I think that at least one bad person definitely *lost*. But now there seem to be two *other* bad people who've turned up and done something bad, and so mummy and her friends are going to have to start all over again chasing *them*. But you're quite right. Mummy wasn't happy today."

"Oh, dear," Rachel said. "It's not good when mummy isn't happy, is it?"

"No," he said, "it's not. But nobody's happy all the time."

Rachel considered this for a moment, and then nodded solemnly.

"Would you like me to read you a story while you start your nap?" he said when they had finished with the dishwasher.

"Yes, please, daddy. The one about the princess and her dog."

"You had that one yesterday."

"It's my favorite. I like it when the princess and her dog are cleverer than her nasty cruel step-father."

"I see. Well then, we'd better have that one."

"I assume," he thought to himself, as the three of them — Rachel, he, and Figaro — climbed the stairs in procession, "that Rachel identifies with the clever princess. And of course Fig will be her clever dog. So who would that make me? I think perhaps I'll just assume I don't come into this story!"

THIRTY-EIGHT

The law offices of Garland, Garland, and Garland in Ropemaker
Street, London EC4. 12:55 p.m., the same day.

The clock on the wall on front of Henry Garland's desk
was the same clock that so far as he knew, with occasional
breaks for cleaning and once, within his memory, for repair and
replacement of some parts, had been ticking away in the office
of the senior partner of the international law firm of Garland,
Garland, and Garland since 1874, including through two world
wars and the Blitz. That same clock now stood at just on five
minutes to one, as his secretary Bob Palmer came into his office
bearing the last will and testament of Jakov Morina, and various papers relating to it.

The firm had, of course, been handling such wills and
bequests regularly throughout the near century and a half of its
existence. Some were last testaments of the famous, some of the
infamous. Into which latter category, Henry Garland reflected,
Jakov Morina undeniably fitted. The will had been properly
drafted—whatever one thought of Jakov Morina personally,
he was no fool—and no one had presumed to challenge it. It
presented no legal problems. But it did, Henry Garland conceded, present what many in the world at large would construe
as surprises.

The first was not particularly surprising to him, because he had handled such final testimonies before. It was simply the fact of how large the estate was: that a convicted felon, serving a life sentence at Her Majesty's pleasure, yet disposed of so much wealth and therefore, even in prison, of so much of the power that goes with wealth.

The second was in the bequests. Most were to family and others who had been loyal to Jakov Morina and his clan. These were to be expected. Even a bequest of half a million pounds to the Greek Orthodox Church, though generous, was not especially surprising. The Morina family was Albanian, and the Albanian Orthodox church was in communion with Constantinople. The Greek Orthodox Church, moreover, had buried Jakov Morina. Therefore his bequest to the Archdiocese of Thyateira and Great Britain was natural enough.

"I dare say the old sinner was hoping to get a few brownie points with Him Upstairs," Bob Palmer said when they first read it through.

"Very probably."

The only condition attached to the bequest was that it was to be anonymous.

"Knowing how he got his money, I expect he thought if they knew where it came from they might feel they'd have to turn it down," Bob Palmer said. "And that'd mean his brownie points with the Almighty would be down the drain and out the window."

Henry Garland nodded, following this tangle of metaphor with an ease that came from thirty years of acquaintance with its source.

"That could well be so," he said.

But the real surprise was in a second bequest, also to a religious institution: a half a million pounds to the sisters of the Community of St. Boniface at St. Boniface Abbey in North Devon, under the same condition of anonymity.

"I do wonder why he'd be leaving his money to an order of Church of England nuns," Henry Garland said.

"I didn't know the Church of England had nuns," Bob Palmer said.

"Oh, it has them all right. But I still can't understand why an Albanian Orthodox crook would be leaving his money to them. There has to be a story behind that!"

"Yes, Mr. Garland."

"Still, as good lawyers, what that story is, we do not need to know. It was his money — well, legally anyway, however ill gotten — so he could leave it to whomever he pleased. I imagine the sisters will do some good with it, and it's none of our business even if they don't. Have you checked everything? All due processes are complete?"

"Yes, Mr. Garland."

"Then I dare say we are all set to announce the good news to the happy inheritors."

The clock on the wall whirred into action and struck one. Henry Garland looked at his watch, as he always did.

"It's getting late," he said, "and I have an appointment at the Arsenal Football Stadium. So let us leave that joyful task until Monday morning. Make it my first priority, will you, Bob?"

"Yes, Mr. Garland. I'll see to it the papers are on your desk."

THIRTY-NINE

After she had left Michael and Rachel, Cecilia did some shopping in Exeter, and then drove back to Edgestow. As was her habit, she took the slower route, by country roads, and so she arrived back in the town at just after three.

She found a car and a large van parked close by the giant trailers that for the past eleven or so weeks had constituted Edgestow's temporary police station. Figures in overalls were unloading office equipment from the van and carrying it into the newly refurbished building — formerly a private hotel — that stood behind the trailers and was destined to be permanent headquarters for the Edgestow Police. Clearly, preparations were nearing completion, which was as well, since Cecilia and her colleagues were scheduled to hand over responsibility for the town to the new force at the end of next week.

She went to the trailer nearest the entrance.

Sergeant Wyatt was at his usual place behind the desk.

"All well, sergeant?"

"Yes, ma'am. Only Joseph's eager to speak with you when you've got a minute."

"Thank you, sergeant. I'll go and see him now."

But then she paused, and nodded towards the window behind him.

"I see they're starting to move in. They should be all set to go when it's time for us to leave, and right on time. Are you looking forward to getting home?"

"Yes ma'am. Not that it hasn't been interesting being in Edgestow! — in fact I wouldn't have missed it. And we've certainly had our bits of excitement. But Mrs. Wyatt will be back from her sister's on Saturday, so it'll be time for me to be home, too."

"Well I've certainly valued your being here, sergeant. You are always a tower of strength and common sense."

"Thank you, ma'am."

"Is Mrs. Wyatt coming straight from Marseilles? That is where her sister lives, isn't it?"

"Yes ma'am — yes to both questions!"

"Well, please give her my best regards when you talk to her, will you?"

"Yes, ma'am. I'll do that."

The sky was overcast and rain was coming in spurts as Cecilia made her way across damp gravel to the other trailer, in part of which they had set up Joseph with his equipment. She found him there with Verity, who was sitting on his desk beside his computer drinking tea from a large blue and white striped mug, her hair rather more disheveled than usual and looking, Cecilia thought, remarkably pretty.

"Joseph, I gather you wanted to see me."

"I wanted to bring you up to date on what we're doing, ma'am."

"Okay."

"First, about Saul Abrahams and Edwin Shale. As I knew you wanted to get on with it, I'm getting a couple of our new blokes back at Heavitree to take a run at them. They're good, I promise you. And they've promised to have whatever they turn up back to me here first thing tomorrow morning. I'll let you have it at once."

Cecilia nodded.

"Good."

"Now, you also asked me to be researching the Morina women, and I've come up with several things that I think will interest you."

"You do know about Shpend Morina being killed last night?"

Verity and Joseph exchanged glances.

Verity smiled.

"We heard this morning," she said. "The thing is, we think we know who did it."

Cecilia pulled out a chair and sat down.

"Fire away," she said.

"Well, ma'am," Joseph said, "what I've been chasing up is mostly about the twins, Mirela and Lule, Ariana's younger sisters."

Cecilia nodded.

"It appears that in 1991, after the noise and flack of the men in the family being tried and sent to prison died down, their mother, Mirela Morina, emigrated to South America. She went to live in San José in Costa Rica, and of course she took the twins Mirela and Lule with her. The twins were then thirteen years old."

Again Cecilia nodded.

"The two girls completed their schooling in San José. Then during the next few years they both went to college there and trained and qualified as nurses. They both married doctors. They now each have two children—no more twins in the family so far, but a boy and a girl each. They've got a Facebook page. Would you like to see it? It's mostly in Spanish, but there are a few bits in English."

"Should I ask how you accessed their Facebook page?" Cecilia asked.

"Probably not," Verity said. "But he means no harm, and they do look nice."

"Actually, they don't even put any limit on who sees their posts," Joseph said. "I don't think they care who looks at it."

So she looked.

Her Spanish was labored, to say the best of it: but she understood enough to see that Mirela Valverde and Lule Madrigal (as they now were, following their respective marriages) had pages filled with the usual kind of good humored Facebook nonsense, with here and there a serious thought about life or the world. To judge from the photographs posted by them and their friends, they were a contented, prosperous group with some serious concerns, delightful looking children, and what seemed overall to be pleasant, useful lives.

"Right," she said.

"One more little detail," Joseph said, "before we get to the interesting stuff. Each of the twins seems to have developed a sporting interest. To be precise, Lule is a motorcyclist. She rides regularly in rallies and road races, and she is very good at it."

Cecilia raised an eyebrow.

"Does she now?"

"Here she is with her motorcycle of choice—having just won the 2011 Motorcycle Tour of Costa Rica."

He brought up the photograph of a dark-haired young woman in black leathers astride a Ducati Panigale 899.

"Mirela her twin sister is not especially interested in motor bike riding, but she is a crack shot with a pistol. She has twice been President of the Sociedad de Armas de San José, and was invited to be part of Costa Rica's 2012 Olympics team. She declined because she said that as a professional nurse and a mother she didn't have the time. Here she is with her weapon of choice."

Another photograph.

"That, I think, is a Glock 42 subcompact pistol that she's holding, isn't it?" Joseph asked.

"It certainly looks like it," Cecilia said.

"Which fires .380 bullets, I gather?"

"It does indeed."

"The kind of bullets that killed Shpend Morina, I believe."

Cecilia smiled, as it was now obvious where all this was going.

"Yes, Joseph."

"Now, in the entire twenty years that have passed since 1993, so far as I can see, Lule and Mirela never once made their way back to England. Neither, incidentally, has their mother, who is still alive and well and also lives in San José, presumably now proud and happy to be a four times grandmother."

"Oh."

"Until this year!"

"Ah!"

"Careful exploration of the airline records for flights to and from San José reveals the Morina twins booked twice on flights to London in the last three months – under their married names, but with absolutely no attempt at secrecy. Incidentally, although all three of them have become citizens of Costa Rica, the twins have evidently kept up their European citizenship too, since they both entered the UK on current, valid British passports, issued and renewed by the British Embassy in San José. Their first arrival in London was on the third of September, which I am sure rings a bell with you."

"They came in good time to be here for their grandfather's funeral on the fifth," Cecilia said.

"Exactly. And we can be sure of that because I've even managed to spot them a couple of times in news shots of the funeral. Obviously, they weren't pushing themselves into the limelight, but they weren't hiding either. There" – he pulled another photograph up onto the computer screen, and pointed to two figures near the back of the group at Jakov Morina's grave-side—"and there"—he indicated another photograph—"that's surely them, on the fringes of the family."

"Agreed," Cecilia said.

"They stayed on in London for two weeks—until the seventeenth, to be exact—no doubt to see London again after all those years, but I dare say they visited their grandfather's grave a few times more."

"And," Verity said, "I think we can guess who they met there on one of those visits."

Cecilia nodded.

How had Chiara remembered Barbara's words?

I saw two people standing there who I had thought were lost to me forever, and I found they still loved me, and we embraced and promised to pray for each other always, even though we may never see each other in this life again.

"It is absolutely brilliant of you both to have put all this together," she said.

"It's Joseph who does it," Verity said. "I just sit here making encouraging noises."

"It's nothing any obsessive compulsive with access to the Internet couldn't manage," Joseph said. "But hang on a minute, there's more."

"I'd love it if your 'more' was that their second visit to England was after Sister Barbara was murdered," Cecilia said.

"Then the genie of the computer shall grant your wish, oh prescient Detective Chief Inspector. That's exactly when it was. They arrived here on Sunday the tenth of November—in excellent time to attend Sister Barbara's funeral on the Tuesday."

Cecilia's mind was racing.

"Don't tell me—wait!—oh, no! There were two young women there from the Associated Press."

"Exactly," Verity said. "We've checked now and of course AP has never heard of them and didn't send anyone to Sister

Barbara's funeral. But on the day of the funeral the two of them had me fooled completely. I thought them completely legit and had a really nice chat with them! But then, I thought the villainous Sir James Harlow was lovely before you nicked him, so what do I know about anything?"

"And they stayed on in England?"

"In London—at the Jumeirah Lowndes Hotel in Lowndes Square," Joseph said, "which is five star, extremely comfortable, and not at all cheap, so they obviously aren't short of a bob or two and believe in doing things properly. Now, here's what's really interesting. They checked out *very* early this morning—well, actually it was the middle of the night, just after midnight, according to the hotel. Everything paid up of course and all quite proper, so they were perfectly entitled to leave any time they liked. But still, they did it suddenly and without any warning at all! They took a limo to Heathrow Airport. On the way there—by Internet from the limo, so far as I can see—they booked themselves onto Iberia Airlines 6:30 a.m. flight from Heathrow to Madrid, and then onto an ongoing Iberia Airlines Flight from Madrid to San José. All first class, of course! They duly left Heathrow on that flight, and then at Madrid caught their connecting trans-Atlantic flight to San José." He glanced at the clock on the wall in front of them. "They will by now have arrived in—"

"She gets it, darling," Verity said.

"Oh. Well then, to sum up: it's during Lule's and Mirela's very last evening in the land of the brave and the free that our friend Shpend, who has murdered their sister, unexpectedly gets his definitive comeuppance from two small slim people, one of whom apparently handles a superbike as if born on it and the other is a crack shot with a light pistol. Just after which, by some strange coincidence, the said Lule and Mirela suddenly pack up their stuff and get out of town in one hell of a hurry!"

Cecilia nodded, then,

"Ah!" she said suddenly. "And now something else that's been puzzling me suddenly makes sense."

The two looked at her.

"The Met report says a DI Sanders who was at the scene heard one of the people on the motorbike say to Shpend, 'Your sister was worth ten of you.' And of course Ariana wasn't Shpend's sister, she was his cousin. But so far as I can gather the DI was running and there was a lot going on. He was still some meters from the corner of the mews and the killer was speaking from inside a full mask crash helmet. So what if what he heard the shooter say wasn't, '*Your* sister,' but '*Our* sister.' There'd be almost no difference in sound."

"Sounds good to me," Verity said.

"Right," Cecilia said. "Congratulations to both of you! This is an absolutely brilliant piece of speculation. I'm totally in awe. And for what it's worth, I think it very likely you're right." She hesitated. "That doesn't mean, of course, that we can do anything about it. Not only does the UK not have an extradition treaty with Costa Rica, even more to the point—"

She paused, inviting them to complete her thought.

"We don't have any evidence," Verity said.

"Exactly."

Joseph nodded.

"Not a shred!" he said cheerfully. "And elegant and persuasive though our conclusions may be, from the strictly legal point of view the complete lack of any evidence to support them *is* a definite drawback!"

FORTY

Edgestow temporary police station. About 4:00 p.m.,
the same afternoon.

Cecilia phoned Chief Superintendent Davies and gave him a summary of Joseph's report.

"I'm sending you the whole thing now," she said, "but that's the gist of it."

"Brilliant work by Joseph," he said, "and it makes perfect sense. Those twins were sent to the best schools in the country, but they also grew up in a family of top class villains. So of course they know what a professional killing looks like. And I dare say they could still call on some of their grandfather's old contacts — folks who'd be quite willing to help them when they made clear who they were and what they were about. The old man inspired loyalty — that's obvious."

"Will you pass Joseph's report on to the Met, sir?"

"Of course."

He paused.

"But," he added, "I'm also sure you're right as to what they or any of us can do about it. There isn't any evidence. If something unexpected were to turn up, like the murder weapon, that would be another matter. But that's a pretty big 'if.' I dare say that particular gun is now safely at the bottom of the Thames.

For our part, I suggest we all move on and concentrate on trying to find out where that painting has gone."

"You're very philosophical about all this, sir."

"Just occasionally, Cavaliere, the best thing we can do about something is to do nothing. I think this may be one of those times. Justice of a kind has been served. It's not our sort of justice and it happens to be against the laws of England. So if we had any evidence against these women and they were available, we'd be bound to prosecute. But as we haven't and there isn't, if there's no prosecution I'm not going to break my heart over it."

"Oh."

Just in time, Cecilia managed to stop herself from saying, for what would have been the second time within a week, "I can't believe you just said that, sir."

Instead, she contented herself with, "Right, sir. I'll let you know if we get anything on the painting."

Her call completed, Cecilia replaced the handset and sat for several minutes gazing out of the window. Above her, bare branches of the trees were silhouetted against a grey, darkening sky. Sergeant Wyatt switched on lights in the other trailer. Lights were going on in upper windows across the way. She sat back in her chair and took a deep breath. There was something about twilight and lights going on that always made her feel slightly voluptuous. She had no idea why.

She decided to phone Michael.

He must have been at his desk, for he answered immediately.

"Do you have time to talk about the case I'm on?" she said.

"Absolutely. I'm about to compose tomorrow's sermon, so perhaps you'll give me inspiration."

"And perhaps I won't. Anyway, thank you."

She told him about Joseph's investigations, and then about her conversation with the chief superintendent, which had left her feeling disturbed and uncomfortable.

"The thing is, you can't believe how often I've heard Glyn Davies say things like, 'In this country there's no place for people who take the law into their own hands — *Make my day!* and all that nonsense! That's not how we do things in the United Kingdom.'"

Michael chuckled.

"What's funny about that?" she said.

"Nothing I know of. It's you. You really do Glyn Davies quite well. Even Glyn Davies taking off Clint Eastwood! And even over the phone!"

"Oh! All right then."

Was she getting over sensitive?

"Well anyway," she said, "I admit that Shpend Morina seems to have been a total waste of space, and I certainly don't mourn his passing. But I can hardly believe it when he's bumped off in a drive-by shooting and then Chief Superintendent Davies of all people sits back and says, 'Perhaps it's all for the best.'"

"In one of Dorothy Sayers's novels," Michael said, "wasn't there a crime where some thoroughly evil person was murdered and Peter Wimsey said, 'Let the justice of God be done,' and refused to investigate?"

"Lord Peter Wimsey was a private detective," Cecilia said. "He could pick and choose what crimes he investigated. We're police officers. We don't have that luxury."

"But isn't that just what Davies said? If there were evidence and the women were available, you'd have to prosecute. But since there isn't and they aren't, he isn't going to break his heart over it. And I can see his point. I mean, if this were a story from antiquity, the brave women who avenged their sister's death by killing the man who'd murdered her might quite possibly be its heroines! The ancients honored fierce women who acted when the men of the clan couldn't — or wouldn't. Think of Judith. Or Jael. Or Electra. And if their sister had vowed her life to a god or goddess, they'd be avenging the god's honor, too. *Autres temps, autres mœurs!* So why are you getting so excited about it? It isn't even your case."

"I'm not quite sure why," Cecilia said. "I suppose, well, I almost get the feeling Davies *admires* these women."

"Perhaps he does. And so?"

"So—I find that disturbing. I feel confused."

"Could it be," he said after another pause, "that your problem is that you rather admire them too, and aren't at all comfortable admitting it?"

"*Me?*"

"Yes. On Saturday you thought the police had been beaten to the punch by a couple of paid professional killers. Which was depressing, but at least straightforward. Now you think they were beaten by a couple of avenging angels. Which isn't at all the same thing."

"Nonsense!" she said.

But then as she spoke, she knew that wasn't true.

"Well, perhaps," she said. "Perhaps I do admire them a bit. But then—isn't that the problem? Should I admire them at all?"

"Why not? However you look at it, there's actually quite a lot to admire. What they did was skillful, audacious, and risky. And they didn't do it for personal gain but as they saw it to redress a wrong. Don't get me wrong. I believe in due process. It *would* have been better if Shpend Morina had been brought to face a judge and a jury. And because they haven't allowed that to happen, what they did is a crime in the eyes of the law. But that doesn't mean there's *nothing* to admire about it."

"I suppose not. But it's confusing."

"It always is when things aren't just plain good or bad—which is most of the time, of course!"

He paused, then said, "And I think maybe this one's especially confusing for you. You've chosen quite deliberately to follow a different path from personal vendetta—and I think for good reason—

His faults lie open to the laws; let them,
Not you, correct him.

—I've heard you quote that more than once. But that doesn't mean that for you personally it's always an easy path. You are proud, brave, and strong. God help the man who had harmed Rachel or your parents if he found himself alone with you and you forgot yourself. I wouldn't fancy his chances."

"Or who had harmed you," she said quietly.

"Or me. Thank you. Or even Figaro!" he said in a slightly lighter tone. "You are after all, and as you remind me from time to time with entirely justifiable pride, a southern Italian."

She laughed. Suddenly she felt better. In fact somewhat elated.

"Or Felix and Marlene!" she said. "He'd better not touch my husband's cats!"

"Exactly."

"Verity says the Welsh do feuds and vendettas as well as the Italians," she said, "and quotes Sir John Somebody-or-other of Somewhere-unpronounceably-Welsh who is a great historian and knows all about it. Come to think of it, maybe she's right. The Chief Superintendent is as Welsh as they come. Maybe that's why he caught onto it so quickly."

"Maybe it is."

"Anyway—I get it. Since there's nothing I can do about it anyway, I don't have to beat myself up because in my heart of hearts I can't help rather admiring a couple of women who gave royal if somewhat bloody comeuppance to the rat who'd murdered their sister. And I don't have to think Glyn Davies has gone over to the dark side if maybe he feels the same."

"As usual, what took me about a thousand words to say, you seem to have covered in about a hundred. Maybe you should become a priest."

"A few weeks ago Verity was telling me I ought to be a soldier. I think I'll stick to being a police officer, thank you. I dare say that's about half way between the two. I think I'd better go now. Did I inspire you for tomorrow's sermon?"

"Probably not."

"Oh. That's not good."

"I'll think of something. When in doubt, exegete the text!"

"I do love you, you know."

"I love you, too."

FORTY-ONE

*Edgestow temporary police station, 4:45 p.m.
the same afternoon.*

Cecilia stayed for some time at her desk working files, dealing with routine emails, and pausing occasionally to gaze at the windows and think about her conversation with Michael. By now it was quite dark outside, and she could see little in the glass but reflections of her own office.

"Ma'am?"

Verity was standing in the doorway.

"Yes, Verity?"

"Joseph's people in Heavitree got the Abrahams and Shale reports over to us by four o'clock, which was sooner than they'd expected. For the last half-hour I've been looking at what they've come up with. You need to hear it."

Cecilia sat back.

"Fire away then."

"Saul Abrahams is straightforward enough, and it all fits with what he told us about himself. It's Edwin Shale who's the surprise."

"Go on."

"First of all, he's Albanian, at least by birth. He changed his name to Edwin Shale by Deed Poll in 2011. Albanian civil

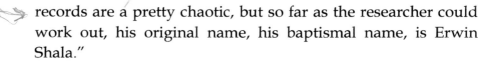

records are a pretty chaotic, but so far as the researcher could work out, his original name, his baptismal name, is Erwin Shala."

Cecilia frowned.

"Wait a minute—Shala? *Shala*? That name's in the Morina file."

"Yes, ma'am. That was Erwin Shala, who was close to Jakov Morina and got jailed with him in 1990. Our Edwin Shale, or Erwin Shala the Second if you like, is his son."

"So he must have grown up with Shpend Morina. He'll have known him for years."

"Right. Now do you remember when we first interviewed him and he said we were welcome to search for the stolen painting in his house or the premises of Clerk and Gregson?— and you said either that meant he was innocent or he'd stashed it somewhere else?"

"I do."

"Well, he owns a house in Clyst Honiton in the name of Edwin Shale. That's what Clark and Gregson has as his home address. But an HM Land Registry search reveals that in the name of Erwin Shala he *also* owns a property in Ottery St. Mary. I don't think it's anything very large, but I bet it's big enough to stash a painting in."

Cecilia nodded.

"I dare say it is," she said.

"Now listen to this, then. After the Morina trial in 1990, Valdete Sala, Erwin's mother, took her son and went back to Albania, where he spent his teens and his early twenties. His English, as we heard, is perfect. I suspect his Albanian is, too. I imagine he's perfectly bilingual, like you. Anyway, he studied for three years in the Faculty of Visual Arts in the University of Arts in Tirana, where his focuses were painting and the history of painting. He graduated in 1996 *summa cum laude* and top of his class in *both* areas. Which means that when I asked him if he painted and he said he had no skills as a painter, he was lying. He *does* have skills, and apparently the faculty of arts thought they were pretty formidable."

"Oh."

"And even that's not all."

Cecilia waited.

"He's currently a member of the British Library — has been since he came back to England. Now one remarkable thing about the British Library, dating back to the years when they were the British Museum Reading Room, is that they keep the most amazing records. And in this case the records tell us that in 2012, while Edwin Shale was working in London, he chose to examine some very interesting documents. One of them was a short history of the Order of St. Boniface, published in 1937. And another was a scruffy little pamphlet called *St. Boniface Abbey in the County of Devon* by someone called The Reverend Septimus Trope, Vicar of All Saints' Church in Edgestow (which isn't there any more — disappeared in the 1945 earthquake, I'm afraid). The pamphlet's undated but the library catalogue notes it as printed '*circa* 1897.' It's basically an inventory of the abbey's treasures. And look. I've highlighted the important bit."

She handed Cecilia a photocopy of a printed page. It listed, as hanging in the abbey library, "a painting of the Blessed Virgin Mary and the Infant Jesus by the Italian artist Giovanni Domenico Tiepolo (1727-1804). This beautiful painting was a gift of Bishop Henry Phillpotts to the Sisters of the Order of St. Boniface at the time of the Order's founding."

Cecilia read it, nodded, and looked up again.

"So," Verity said, "it looks to me as if Shale was *also* lying when he told us that before he started his evaluation at the abbey he expected the painting Bishop Phillpotts had given them to be by a Victorian nonentity! If he'd read Trope's pamphlet, then he knew that at least one observer said it was a Tiepolo. What he didn't know, I imagine, was exactly where it was. He'd have no reason to think it wasn't still in the library. But then, of course, he'd have learned its true whereabouts when he did the evaluation."

Cecilia gave a soft whistle.

"Right!" she said. "Top marks to everybody. And now we need to act." She looked at her watch. "The chief super should still be in his office. While I'm getting on to him, sort out a good driver—preferably someone who likes driving at night!—and our fastest car, will you?" She stopped. "Are you all right, Verity?"

"Yes ma'am, sort of—I mean, I really hate this."

"I know. It's awful when you like them. All I can say is, I've been there. And I'm sorry."

"Thank you, ma'am. And don't worry—I'll do my job. I think the driver will be Jarman, and the Volvo's the fastest we've got here."

"Tell Jarman to get prepared to drive it, then. I think Davies may want us at the center for this."

While Verity went to find PC Jarman, Cecily stabbed in the chief superintendent's number.

FORTY-TWO

Heavitree Police Station, Exeter. A few minutes later.

Davies's reaction when Cecilia phoned and told him the news was swift.

"Right," he said, "hang on, Cavaliere."

He buzzed his secretary.

"Tell Inspector Coyle I need him in here on the double."

"Yes, sir."

"Cavaliere?"

"Sir?"

"I'm sending uniform to all three addresses to find Shale now. Since he misled you and DS Jones, that alone gives us grounds to bring him in for questioning. By all means get yourselves on the road, but make sure you stay in communication. I may want to give you fresh instructions."

By the time Inspector Coyle and three other officers arrived at Ottery St. Mary, they already knew that their fellow officers had failed to find Shale at the premises of Clark and Gregson or at his home in Clyst Honiton.

He was not to be found at Ottery St. Mary either. The property was a large barn converted into a studio. There were canvases, paints, easels, and all the usual tools of the artist's trade. They found Karrimo Tempo trainers under a table, and a drawer with several pairs of leather gloves, all of which they placed into evidence bags. They had with them a photograph of the missing painting, and they found what looked like preliminary sketches for a copy of it. But the painting itself they did not find. Nor did they find Erwin Shale.

But then a sharp-eyed constable did discover something of interest in a waste paper basket.

"Look at this, sir," she said to Inspector Coyle.

He looked at it, and then at his watch.

"Well done!" he said. "Thanks to you I think we just got lucky."

He called Heavitree.

"Sir," he said to Chief Superintendent Davies a few minutes later, "Shale's obviously done a runner from here too. But PC Baron has found a receipt for an airline e-ticket in the waste paper basket. It looks as if Shale's booked himself on a 5:45 p.m. flight from Bristol to Berlin. But it surely won't have taken off yet? So they could hold it, couldn't they?"

"I'll get onto them," the chief superintendent said.

When the man in charge of operations at Bristol Airport received the call from Heavitree Police Station he seemed inclined to demur.

"The passengers have already been checked through security and onto the plane, it's taxiing and is about to be cleared for takeoff. I really can't hold it up now."

"You mean it's physically impossible to stop it taking off?"

"Well no, of course it's not physically impossible. It's in contact with air traffic control. But it's a scheduled flight and it's on the runway. It will cause chaos. You people don't know what you're asking."

"Well then," Davies said, "let me tell you what I *do* know. Officers from Exeter CID will be with you shortly — probably about an hour. They will of course know that I have requested your assistance in this matter. At which point one of two things will happen. Either you will have held that flight so they can board it and arrest their man, or they will arrest *you* for failure to assist a police office in making an arrest, for obstructing the police in the course of their duties and, since the suspect is wanted for questioning in connection with murder and a major art theft, quite possibly as accessory after the fact in the matter of those crimes too. Do I make myself clear?"

There was a pause.

"I'll get air traffic control to hold the flight," the controller said.

"Good man," Davies said. "I thought you might."

Davies replaced the phone and smiled. Refusing to assist a constable in making an arrest had, as he happened to know, been an offence under English and Welsh common law since the Middle Ages. To be sure, he wasn't aware of anyone actually being prosecuted for it during the last five hundred or so years — but that, clearly, did not mean that as a law it didn't still have its uses!

The Chief Superintendent came through on Cecilia's mobile.

"Where are you?"

"Passed through Tedburn St. Mary about five minutes back, sir."

"How quickly can you get to Bristol Airport?"

She looked at Jarman.

"From here via the motorway," he said, "if I keep the siren and the emergency lights going, and the traffic stays light, I reckon about seventy minutes. Maybe even a bit less."

"Go for it," Davies said. "They'll be expecting you."

***

Cecilia always found airports exciting, and especially so at night. She felt her pulse quicken as the Volvo, siren still blaring and emergency lights flashing, left the A38 via the airport roundabout and was waved past car parks and on towards the terminal. Of course Bristol was hardly Heathrow or Gatwick, but still it had something of the exotic, and especially so when linked to a floodlit runway and banks of beacons and signals. Jarman pulled alongside the brightly lit terminal building, where two Avon and Somerset Constabulary vehicles with lights flashing were already parked—a Land Rover and a police van. Several uniformed police officers were grouped near the main entrance, and as Cecilia got out of the Volvo, one of them left the group and came across to her.

"Good evening," he said. "I'm Inspector Cardin of the Bristol Airport Police. I take it you are Detective Chief Inspector Cavaliere of Exeter CID and Detective Sergeant Jones?"

"That's us," Cecilia said.

"I understand you're to make an arrest. We're here to assist in any way you need. Your suspect's flight is being held in an area by the runway, so we can take you to it whenever you're ready. After you've made the arrest we've a van here that can take him to Exeter for you. Your Chief Superintendent Davies also asked us to remove the suspect's luggage from the aircraft, and we've done that. He thought you'd want to take a look at it before you made the arrest."

Clearly, Chief Superintendent Davies had not been letting the grass grow under his feet.

"Thank you, Inspector," Cecilia said. "Let's go and look at the luggage then."

He led them to a room off the baggage claim area, where they were faced with two unusually shaped wooden boxes, each about ten centimeters deep, one of them something over a meter square, the other about half that size.

"Definitely out-of-size baggage!" Cardin said.

"These would presumably have been checked by security?"

"For drugs, weapons, and explosives, yes."

"And beyond that?"

Cardin went over to a computer and checked it.

"The paperwork was in order, prepared by a reputable company of antique valuers, dealers, exporters and importers, and the description appeared to match the contents—oil paintings on canvas, framed, one in each container, each insured for one thousand pounds. So they let them through."

"And let me guess—the reputable company was Clark and Gregson of London and Exeter?"

Cardin peered again at the computer.

"That's right," he said.

Cecilia exchanged a glance with Verity. "Than I think we can guess how that was managed."

"Shall we open them for you?" he asked.

"Yes," Cecilia said, "but being very careful! If they are what I think they are, they're oil paintings on canvas all right, but worth a whole lot more than a thousand pounds each."

Cardin nodded to two constables, who between them managed without much difficulty to remove one of the ends from the smaller of the two boxes, then to remove some padding, and finally to slide out what it contained, which was wrapped in sheets of bubble wrap.

One of them looked up at Cecilia, who nodded.

He carefully cut the sheets of bubble wrap and pulled them back. Then he removed a thin board that sat on the frame, protecting the painted canvas.

He gazed down at it for a moment, then lifted the framed canvas, placed it against the wall, and stepped away so that the others could see.

Everyone gave a slight, involuntary gasp.

One of the constables crossed himself.

Gazing at them, serene and full of grace, were the Blessed Virgin and her Child.

As they were being driven across the runway towards the waiting aircraft, Verity turned to Cecilia.

"Ma'am, I'd like to make a request."

"What's that, Verity?"

"Ma'am, I know you're the senior investigating officer. But in this case, if you don't think it inappropriate, may I make the arrest?"

"Since you made the connections that led up to it, I think that for you to make the arrest will be entirely appropriate, Detective Sergeant Jones. Please do that."

FORTY-THREE

Easyjet Flight 6237 to from Bristol to Berlin, Schonefeld Airport.

The stewardess standing by the door of the Airbus 320 smiled and said, "Good evening" to Verity as she entered.

"Good evening," Verity replied — both of them, she reflected, scrupulously maintaining normal professional courtesies.

Verity signaled to the uniformed police officers behind her to follow, and entered the aircraft, walking past the stewardess to the head of the passenger cabin. At their appearance the soft buzz of conversation that had preceded it died. Rows of faces gazed at them, some curious, some surprised, some irritated, some intrigued, and most, she thought, merely tired.

Among them, after a moment, she saw Edwin Shale: seated near the back, leaning out into aisle to see what was going on. He was rubbing his eyes. Perhaps he had dozed off, bored with waiting, until something about their entry — a sound, or even the very silence and change of mood that followed it — caused him to wake.

And now he had seen her. Their eyes met. For an instant his registered delighted surprise — delight that turned in another instant to horror, as he surely realized there could be only one reason why she was there. She walked slowly toward him, conscious of the uniformed officers who followed her and, behind them, of Cecilia.

And now she was standing by him, looking down. He gazed up at her.

"I really didn't want this to be you," she said quietly.

"I know," he said. "I'm sorry."

She nodded.

"Edwin Shale," she said, "alias Ervin Shala, I am arresting you in connection with the murder of Sister Barbara of the Order of Saint Boniface on the night of the fifth of November 2013, and for the theft of paintings from the Courtauld Institute of Art in London on the seventh of June 2012, and from St. Boniface Abbey on the fifth of November 2013. You do not have to say anything. But it may harm your defence if you do not mention when questioned something which you later rely on in court. Anything you do say may be given in evidence."

He gave a wry smile.

"Well," he said, "I will say one thing, whether it's given in evidence or harms my defence or anything else. I want *you* to know I had nothing to do with the death of that poor woman. I was there to get the painting. Shpend Morina told me he was going to talk with his cousin, and when I left them, talking is what they were doing. I assumed she was in on the whole thing. I didn't even know she was dead until I saw it on television. That is God's truth, on my life."

Verity nodded.

"You will have the services of a lawyer, Mr. Shale. If you can persuade the Crown Prosecution Service that you knew nothing of Sister Barbara's death, I imagine that part of the charges against you may be dropped. Although of course it's not up to me to say."

She had already decided that if he made it possible, she would exercise the discretion allowed to arresting police officers in the United Kingdom and spare him at least one indignity. So she asked, "Will you come with us quietly, Mr. Shale?"

"Yes of course."

"Good. Then we don't need to use handcuffs."

She turned to the uniformed officer behind her.

"Constable."

"Yes, ma'am."

She walked a couple of paces further down the aisle, then turned and watched as her place was taken by the officer, who instructed Shale to unfasten his seatbelt, then gently but firmly brought him to his feet, taking care as he did so to ensure that Shale did not bang his head against the overhead luggage compartments.

"It's been a night of rushing about for all of you, but a good result," Davies said when it was all over and Cecilia called him from the car. "Are you lot up to driving back to Exeter now and spending the night here? It would be good if you and Jones could question Shale here formally tomorrow morning."

She looked at the others.

Jarman said, "No problem as far as I'm concerned. I'll stay with my mum."

"I'll be glad of a quiet night in my own flat," Verity said.

"It looks like we're all good for it," Cecilia said to Davies.

"Good. Well let's say you and DS Jones question Shale here at ten o'clock tomorrow morning."

"Do I get to use the siren and the emergency lights again on the way back to Exeter?" Jarman asked as they prepared to leave the airport.

"No, constable," Cecilia said, "you don't. I grant they are enormously satisfying. I simply *love* seeing everything scatter to get out of our way! But the word 'emergency' means, oddly enough, 'emergency.' We shall proceed calmly and unobtrusively, as befits sober guardians of the law who are not in any particular hurry."

He grinned.

"Right you are, ma'am. Before we start, though, if you don't mind I'll just phone mum. Let her know I'm coming."

"That will be fine, constable."

FORTY-FOUR

Old Abbey Court, Salmon Pool Lane, Exeter.
Verity Jones's flat.

When Verity said she'd be glad of a night alone in her flat, she thought she meant it. It wasn't that she regretted having asked to arrest Edwin Shale. She felt that she owed him that. But actually doing it had felt like beating a willing pony or an affectionate dog. She felt terrible. She needed time alone to recoup, to regroup.

Except that it hadn't worked like that. She had misread her own needs. Cecilia and PC Jarman brought her to her front door and left her, and now she was alone and hated it. Normally she loved her little flat, but tonight everything about it that was usually warm and comforting seemed alien and sterile.

Everywhere she looked, she seemed to see the frightened eyes of Edwin Shale.

Finally she telephoned Joseph at his digs in Edgestow. She gathered he was getting ready for bed, but he seemed pleased that she had called.

"How did everything go?" he asked — he knew that she and Cecilia had set off from Edgestow in pursuit of Shale.

"It went well. And it was horrible," she said, and then to her surprise and irritation started to cry.

"Verity!" he said, "Darling! What on earth's the matter?"

She pulled herself more or less together and told him what had happened. All of it: how she and Cecilia had first gone to see Edwin Shale and questioned him, and how he had helped her see the French painting properly, and how he'd phoned and asked her to go to the theatre with him. And then how it turned out that he'd lied to them about being a painter, and lied to them about what he knew about what was in the abbey. Everything.

"So when I arrested him I felt like an evil witch, and he looked up at me like a hurt spaniel. And darling, I know it's ridiculous. I barely know the man. I've only spoken with him three times in my life — and of those one was on the phone and another was to arrest him! But I like him! He seems nice. Except that he's this terrible crook. But I'm engaged to you. I oughtn't to be feeling like this. It's all so illogical. If I make this big a mess of being a fiancée, how on earth will I manage as a wife?"

"You're losing me. I thought we were talking about Shale. How have you made a mess of being a fiancée? Because you like Shale? Or because he likes you?"

"I don't know. Both! Any of it!"

"If I thought being engaged meant no other man would ever fancy my fiancée, it was a bit daft of me to get engaged to a woman who's an absolute knockout, wasn't it? And if married love means each of us stopping the other from liking anyone else, that doesn't seem to me to say much for married love."

"Maybe not. I don't know."

"Surely what matters at the end of the day is that we know who *we* are? There's a whole world out there, and we're both free agents. Given that, the only question that I care about is, do you want to be with me?"

"Oh yes! I do! More than anything in the world!"

"And I want to be with you. You're the love of my life. So that's the thing. Everything else must take its place round that.

I'm really sorry you had a horrible day. But I'm *proud* of you, too. You did your duty. And it was all the more honorable because it was a rotten duty."

"*I could not love thee half so much, loved I not honour more.*"

"I believe you. You'd have made a wonderful cavalier lady. The cavaliers would probably have won if you'd been there."

"You do talk nonsense."

"Part of the charm of being married to me will be that you'll get to hear me talk it all the time."

"As Lord Peter Wimsey said to Harriet Vane!"

"And as he also said, I like to have a quotation for everything—it saves me the trouble of thinking!"

"Oh, Joseph, I do wish you were here."

"Be careful what you wish for, Verity!"

She looked at the clock. It was almost midnight.

"Thank you for being so patient and listening to all this and putting up with an idiot. I'll let you go now. I'm all right, I think. And I do love you."

"And I love you, too. Good night. God bless you, my darling."

"God bless you."

About ninety minutes later Verity's phone, which was on the bedside table, suddenly lit up and played its little tune.

She jerked herself awake and fumbled for it.

It was Joseph.

"Joseph! Are you all right? Is something wrong?"

"Nothing's wrong. I'm fine. It's just, well, you know you said earlier you wished I was there? And I said you ought to be careful what you wished for? Well—"

She pushed the phone aside, jumped out of bed, and rushed to the window. There was his car, royal blue, glistening with raindrops under the streetlight.

She could still hear his voice from the phone—"Verity? Are

you still there?" — but she was already through the bedroom door.

In the frosted glass of the front door she could see his silhouette.

She flew down the stairs, opened the door — he still had his phone in his hand — pulled him inside, and shut the door.

"Oh, Joseph!" she said, and clung to him.

"I'm a bit wet," he said. "It's raining."

"I don't care. I like you wet."

She was so happy she thought her heart would break.

FORTY-FIVE

St. Mary's Church, Exeter.

Cecilia went to the 8:00 a.m. celebration. The gospel was all about being questioned by kings and governors and not making up your answers ahead of time, which seemed appropriate enough on a day when she was about to interview a suspect. The only problem was, it only gave advice to the people being questioned. That was all well and good, but she'd have appreciated a word or two about what to do if you happened to be the one doing the questioning.

In general Cecilia liked Michael's sermons. He preached with gentle, often self-deprecating humor that she enjoyed, and had at the same time a gift for explaining difficult texts and ideas. That said, his sermon this morning was not, she thought, up to his usual standard. Presumably this was the one for which she had not inspired him.

But then as she was leaving church she overheard one of the churchwardens, Mr. Oakley, a retired major of the Royal Marines: a pleasant, kindly man, but generally rather reserved. He was talking to Michael at the west door.

"Many thanks for your good words this morning, padre. They were exactly what I needed to hear."

She shrugged mentally. So much for the value of her opinion!

***

The chief superintendent met them by the interview room, obviously intending to observe. They exchanged brief good-mornings.

Inside, Shale was already waiting for them, accompanied by his solicitor — one Mr. Soames, whose competence and professionalism Cecilia had experienced on other occasions. She nodded approvingly. Shale would not, it appeared, lack the best in his counsel.

When Cecilia and Verity entered, Shale rose to his feet, hastily followed by Soames, who was as evidently unused to this courtesy by male prisoners towards female police officers as was Cecilia herself. She nodded to them to sit, and she and Verity took their places opposite.

Cecilia led the questioning. The first thing they wanted to hear about was Edwin Shale's relationship with Shpend Morina.

"Our family had been clients of the Morinas for generations," he said. "So of course I knew them all. My father was close to old Jakov. I grew up calling old Jakov 'grandfather' — even though we weren't related. And Jakov was always kind to me. He said I had talents. Actually, he said one day I'd be an artist."

"You knew Shpend Morina, then?"

"Of course, along with knowing all the others, but not as a friend or anything like that. He a good deal older than me — a man and a grownup! I was just a boy."

After the men of the Morina family together with Shale's father were all arrested and sentenced to prison, Shale's mother took the boy with her back to Albania, where there were still members of the Shala family living, although the Morinas had all left.

"Grandfather Jakov had been very generous. We had plenty of money and so we were able to live comfortably."

"So now you were Albanian again?"

"Yes. I grew up there, completed my education. And grandfather Jakov was right. I became an artist.

"But then in 2011 I had a communication from Shpend Morina in London. There was money to be made, he said—a great deal of money! Even by painters and artists! And he needed my talents. He reminded me of how much I owed his family and his grandfather—which of course was true—and that the Shalas had been clients of the Morinas for generations. So that it seemed to be my duty to come when he called. And I came."

Once Shale had arrived in London, Shpend Morina got him to accept a position in the London branch of Clark and Gregson. Then, on the basis of information obtained by Shale in the course of his work there, they between them organized the theft of the Renoir from the Courtauld Institute in 2012.

"I'd studied it closely during our evaluation processes, and I was convinced—indeed I *am* convinced—that I could make very good copies of it—copies that would fool anyone except an expert, and even some experts. After all, I know what experts look for!

"After that, Morina told me to apply for a move to Clark and Gregson's Exeter branch, which I did—successfully. I purchased properties in Devon, in my English name, and the studio in my Albanian name, which you know about. There we kept the Renoir and there, in time, there would be leisure for me to copy it. But first Morina said, there was one other place where he wanted us to look—to see if there was anything of merit. St. Boniface Abbey, in north Devon."

At which time, Cecilia reflected, Morina knew that his cousin was one of the sisters there. But did he also know of the painting? Before she could put the question, however, Shale was offering an answer to it.

"He had me research the place while I was still in London: which I did, mostly at the British Library. And that's when we discovered—well, *I* discovered and I told him—that they likely had a Tiepolo Madonna. So then, as soon as I got here at the beginning of this year, Morina had me write to the sisters in my capacity as an agent of Cark and Gregson offering a free evaluation of any antiques or works of art they might possess. When I did the evaluation I saw the Tiepolo for the first time, and it broke my heart. Giovanni Domenico Tiepolo was a fine artist. But as regards this particular work I meant what I said last week when you came to see me."

"You said a lot of things, Mr. Shale," Cecilia said, "and not all of them were true. So remind me. What was it you said that you meant?"

"It's a vision of the holy. I wept before it. And I saw how it moved the sisters to prayer. In a way the whole thing was ridiculous. Here was a treasure that would fetch hundreds of thousands of pounds in the art market. Yet scarcely anyone knew where it was or what it was. It was not insured, other than for a few hundred pounds in the general insurance for the whole building. And it wasn't really protected. The sisters treated it with enormous respect, of course, and took great care of it. And conditions in the meditation room are actually quite well suited to its preservation. But they did those things because of what the painting *meant* to them, because for them it was a window into the divine, and not at all because of its financial value, which they hadn't even considered! It was absurd. And yet in another way it was magnificent. It was surely what art was meant to be."

"So what happened then?"

"I gave them an honest appraisal and pressed them to insure it properly. I suppose I knew Shpend would want us to steal it, but at least I intended to see that they didn't lose by it."

"Except," Verity said, looking up from her notes and speaking for the first time, "their window into the divine. They'd lose that, wouldn't they, Mr. Shale? However much money they got? And as you just pointed out, that was actually the only thing they cared about, wasn't it?"

He looked at her and nodded.

"Yes," he said. "You're right. I didn't let myself think of that."

Verity raised her eyebrows, and went back to her notes.

"What happened next, Mr. Shale?" Cecilia asked.

"I did the appraisal in May. For two or three months, nothing happened. Then in early in September Shpend called me, said he was almost ready to act, and there would soon be a chance to take the painting."

Cecilia nodded. So by that point, then, Morina had planned a double operation. He'd kill his cousin and he'd get the Madonna at one stroke.

"Go on."

"A few more weeks passed — then, on the fifth of November Morina called me again. I was to meet him in Edgestow at The Great Western pub that evening. It was all set up. One of the sisters at the abbey was a member of his family — his cousin. She would meet us in the grounds and I would be able to slip in and take the painting. So I did as instructed. I met him at The Great Western. Actually, it was a bit weird, that part."

Cecilia raised an eyebrow, and waited.

"Well, he seemed for a while to be in no particular hurry, but then, suddenly out of the blue, he says 'Drink up!' — though he's only brought us fresh drinks a few minutes earlier! — 'It's time to go!' So I drank up, and he actually poured the rest of his beer into a plant beside our booth. As I say, weird! But I suppose I was too preoccupied with what we were about to do to ask questions. Anyway, then we left."

Cecilia raised an eyebrow and glanced at Verity, who gave a slight nod.

"Did you try to keep yourself unobserved, out of sight, while you were in The Great Western?"

"Certainly I did. We were about to commit a major theft and I have to live round here!"

"So then what happened?"

"We drove out to the abbey, and parked. We were in separate cars, you understand. He'd found a way to get over the wall, which was easy enough, and we met the nun, Sister Barbara, in the grounds under the trees. She seemed to expect us, so I supposed that meant she must be in on it. I admit I was surprised. I mean, I'd met her before when I did their appraisals. She didn't seem at all the type for this kind of thing. I'd found her gracious, even saintly—and I mean that in the best possible way. I *liked* her. But there she was. She obviously knew Shpend and he knew her."

"Describe their meeting more for me, Mr. Shale. What happened? What did they say to each other?"

"Well, as I said, it was as if she expected us—or, at least, she expected him. I mean, we came on her alone in the dark—it was a fine enough night but there was no more than a sliver of moon—yet she didn't seem at all surprised to see us or scared or anything. She said—and I think this is pretty well verbatim—'Hello Shpend. I've been wondering when you'd come! I see you've brought someone with you!' And he said, 'Just an old friend of the *family*, Ariana.' I remember he emphasized 'family,' because it sounded odd. And then he said, 'But he's got a job to do, so I'm afraid he must leave us now.' He'd already told me that she and he had business, and obviously, whatever it was they had to talk about, they—or at least he—didn't want me around. So I said something like, 'Right, I'll see you back in town,' and left them."

"And that was it?"

"Well, there was one other thing. As I was leaving I heard Sister Barbara say, 'I want you to know, Shpend, I forgive you for what you're going to do from the bottom of my heart.' I was going away from them, and her voice was soft, but I think that's what she said. I assumed at the time she meant our stealing the painting, although I realized afterwards—well, it wasn't just that, was it? She *knew* what he was going to do, didn't she?"

"And she appeared to be quite calm for the whole time?"

"Calm, yes. There we were, two biggish men alone with her in the dark, and she was just a tiny little thing, and yet somehow it felt as if she was the strong one. If I had to put a word on her at all, I'd say if anything she seemed sorry for him. Does that make any sense?"

"So you left them and then what?"

"I kept on between the trees—it was easy enough to keep straight, as they're in dead straight rows, and even with a sliver of moon it's surprising how your eyes adjust. I came to the main building, and I stole the painting. Which was hardly a challenge. I knew exactly where it was. The main door wasn't even locked. The other sisters were all, presumably, in bed—certainly there was no sign of them. There was no alarm system of any kind, and the painting wasn't even fastened to the wall, just hanging from it on a hook, as if it was a family-photograph!"

Which for the sisters, in a way, it was, Cecilia thought.

"At one point I heard a dog bark from somewhere in the building, which gave me pause for a moment. I was all set to leg it. But then nothing happened. Clearly nobody took the slightest notice."

"So?"

"So I took the Tiepolo, and I went back through the grounds and over the wall the way we'd come. Shpend had obviously already left—as I assumed, having finished his business with his cousin. His car was gone. I put the painting into my own car and drove to my place at Ottery St. Mary where I left it with the Renoir. We'd already agreed I'd lay low for a few days. Then Shpend was to get in touch with me from London."

He paused and let out a deep sigh.

"But then, the next day, I saw on the news that Sister Barbara had been murdered. I was stunned. And appalled. She was a good lady. And if Shpend had done it—and he surely had—then I'd had a part in her death!"

A good lady! That was what Jennifer Pettigrew said.

"I was also scared. I was scared of what Shpend might do to me if I let on to anybody what I knew, and I was scared of finding myself on trial for murder—especially after you two came round asking questions and it was clear I was a suspect. As how could I not be? I'd always been quite ready to bluff my way through an accusation of art theft—but not murder, for God's sake!"

Again he sighed.

"About a week went by. Some of the time I almost persuaded myself that if I kept my head down and did nothing it would all blow over. But then at other times I'd work myself into a total panic. When would Shpend call me? What would he say or tell me to do when he did? Then I switched on the television yesterday morning and learnt that Shpend himself had been murdered! Shot dead in the street in a drive-by shooting as if London was Los Angeles or Chicago! I have to admit—for a moment I was actually glad. I realized I'd become terrified of the man. But then I began to think about it. Who had he stirred up? Would they be after me next? And I panicked. I decided to get out. I managed to book myself onto that flight to Berlin, spent the morning packing the two paintings and faking valuations and export papers for them—it was easy enough, I had all the proper Clark and Gregson forms and know exactly what you need to say on them—and caught the flight. But then you caught me."

"And these are the two stolen paintings that you tried to export?" Cecilia passed him two photographs, which she identified for the benefit of the recording.

"Yes," he said.

"And what did you intend to do if we hadn't caught you, Mr. Shale?"

"I intended to go back to Tirana, resume my old identity as

Ervin Shala, and set myself up in my old studio. There I would copy the paintings at leisure.

The Renoir I would have copied to make money. The Madonna and Child I would have copied for love."

"Not for money?"

"I would like to paint something that moved people to adoration, to see the presence of God. Tiepolo's Madonna does that. I would have tried to follow it."

"If that's what you wanted," Verity said, "why not just a paint a Madonna for yourself? Why copy someone else's?"

"Because I know my own inadequacy. I am not a master. That was the essential truth in my saying to you when you first interviewed me that I have no skills as a painter and couldn't paint a decent picture. Compared with Tiepolo when he painted that Madonna and Child, or even Renoir when he painted the nude, I haven't and I couldn't."

Verity pursed her lips.

"Given the record of your studies at university, Mr. Shale," she said, "and faculty's opinion of your work there, you must forgive me if your 'essential truth' sounds to me remarkably like what in most circumstances I would call a lie."

"I can see why you would feel that," he said. "And I'm sorry."

"It isn't a question of what I feel, Mr. Shale. The essence of a lie, as I understand the word and as I intended it just now, is that it is a false statement intended to deceive. Did you or did you not intend to deceive us when you said you had no skills as a painter?"

Shale mumbled.

"What was that Mr. Shale?"

"Yes."

"Yes, you intended to deceive us?"

"Yes. I intended to deceive you."

"As you also intended to deceive us when you said you had

no idea there was a painting by Tiepolo in the abbey before you saw it?"

"Yes."

Verity nodded, then went back to her notes.

"So," Cecilia said, "if I'm hearing you correctly Mr. Shale, you confess to having stolen or been involved in stealing two paintings, a Renoir nude from the Courtauld Institute and a Tiepolo Madonna and Child from the Sisters of St. Boniface, but you deny any involvement in Sister Barbara's murder or even knowledge of it until after the fact?"

"Yes."

"When you last saw Sister Barbara, she was alive and well, and talking to Shpend Morina?"

"Yes."

"And you did not see her again?"

"No."

"Do you have any further questions for Mr. Shale, DS Jones?"

"No ma'am."

Cecilia nodded and looked up at the clock, said, "Interview terminated at 11:03"and, stretching across the table, switched off the recording equipment. "You are with me, Detective Sergeant Jones."

"Yes, ma'am."

But then, as they were leaving, Verity turned back in the doorway.

"You know," she said, "when I read your file, Mr. Shale, I saw what the head of the faculty of arts said about you as a student. You were the most brilliant technician with a brush he'd ever worked with. And you had gifts of imagination that he found quite extraordinary, especially considering your youth. So I think that your problem—and your tragedy, unless you change your attitude—isn't at all your inadequacy, or that you haven't the ability to become a master. Your problem is you *may* have that ability, and that's a responsibility you aren't willing to face."

He stared up at her for a moment as she stood looking down at him. Then, slowly, he nodded.

"If ever I have the chance again," he said at last, "I believe I must try. My only excuse so far is—up until now I had not seen my eighteenth century Madonna to inspire me. Now I have. I shall hold on to that memory."

Later, when they were drinking tea together in the cafeteria, Verity said, "Well, it looks as if living with the sisters' painting for a while did do Edwin Shale some good. It seems to have inspired him to try to be what he can be in his own right."

Cecilia nodded but said nothing.

Verity was surely right that in her brief exchange with him Shale had promised that in future he would try to take seriously his own talent. But Cecilia had been watching his eyes and his body language as he made that promise.

Was the "eighteenth-century Madonna" he had now seen, whose memory was henceforth to inspire him, really the sisters' painting?

That, she doubted.

Forty-Six

Bella Italia in Queen Street, Exeter.
A little past noon, the same day.

The restaurant was packed, as it usually was at lunchtime on Sundays, and Cecilia was grateful when she saw Michael waving at her from a corner, having already secured a table.

"Where's Rachel?"

"With your mama and papa at Cricklepit Mill," he said. "There's some special event on and so it's having a Sunday opening — I think it's to do with otters. They took her off straight after church. Then they'll go to the quay and feed the swans and Rachel will have an ice cream with cherries and nuts and bits of chocolate and other wonderful things in it."

"*Ice cream on the quay?* It's 9 degrees Celsius!"

"Who cares about that when you're three years old?"

They ordered.

"So how are we feeling about the state of freedom and democracy this morning?" he asked.

She shook her head.

"Shale was completely cooperative. Of course a lot of what he told us we already knew or guessed. But he's also helped us join up some dots. I suppose what's most important is that he absolutely denies having any part in killing Sister Barbara, and

I believe him. He's a crook but he isn't a murderer. The scene-of-crime evidence supports his version of events. And it isn't as if we don't know who killed her. So I rather imagine CPS will drop that part of the charges. That will be our recommendation, anyway."

"How was Verity?"

"She was fine. Didn't say much, but then a couple of times when she did say something she really nailed him. Indeed, at one point she was quite ruthless. And I think it was the more powerful for him precisely because he knows she likes him." She sighed. "The fact is, he seems a thoroughly nice man—funny, modest, intelligent—everything a man should be. Apart from the fact that he's a criminal. It's depressing."

Michael nodded.

"Someone with that much appreciation of beauty and such eagerness and ability to share it must have a lot of good in him. Poor fellow."

"Exactly. And Shpend Morina was his incubus. So—to answer your question, my feelings about the state of freedom and democracy this morning seem precisely opposite to what they should be. The Morina killing was from a policing point of view something of a disaster, yet I end up feeling quite good about it and even—following my little chat with you—willing to admit it. With the art thefts we have on paper a really good result, and of course I'm glad the sisters will get their Madonna and Child back, but despite all that I end up feeling depressed."

She paused, then added, "*For what we lack,*
We laugh, for what we have we are sorry, still
Are children in some kind."

"Shakespeare?"

"*The Two Noble Kinsmen.* And contrary to what people say about Prospero's farewell speech in *The Tempest*, that may *actually* be the last thing he wrote for the stage. His real farewell."

Michael nodded.

"It sounds almost like Montaigne," he said.

There was a pause in conversation while the waiter brought their antipasti — *insalata fagioli* for Cecilia and *crostini salami* for Michael — and then further moments of silence while they both sampled their food.

"How is it?"

"Actually it's quite good. And yours?"

"Good."

Cecilia told him about Verity's final words with Shale.

"He says," she said, "that when he gets the chance he means to paint seriously from now on, and perhaps he does."

"I suppose he will have to go to prison though, won't he?"

"I imagine so. Given he's non-violent and he's been very co-operative since his arrest, with luck he'll get Category D."

"That's what people call an 'open prison,' isn't it?"

"Right," she said. "But it will still be terrible for a man like him. He'll find himself tied daily, indeed hourly, to a regimen that will seem to him utterly pettifogging and futile. He'll be with people who haven't the slightest interest in art or beauty or anything in the world that he cares about. He'll feel utterly damned and forsaken. And I'm sorry for it."

Michael gave a deep sigh. "Poor fellow. I'll pray for him."

There was a pause.

It was Michael who ended it.

"Dante found himself lost in a dark forest," he said, "but he got to Paradise in the end."

Cecilia gave a sad little smile.

"So he did," she said. "But from where he was he still had to go through hell and purgatory first!"

"And he had the memory of Beatrice to sustain him."

"Maybe Shale has something like that."

"Really?"

"I think he's in love with Verity."

"*Really?*"

"When he said that from now on he meant to work seriously, he also said that from now on he'd have the memory of his eighteenth century Madonna to inspire him. Verity thought he was talking about the Tiepolo painting. But I was watching him. He was talking about her."

Michael raised his eyebrows.

"I admire Verity very much," he said, "but she's hardly a Madonna, eighteenth century or any other sort!"

"He was talking about her appearance — her *looks*. Haven't you noticed? She's like those portraits of Madame de Pompadour: the same kind of features. It's those beautiful cheekbones. Dress her in the right clothes and she'd fit in perfectly at the court of Louis XV. Which is exactly what a painter like Shale would notice."

"But Shale hardly knows her."

Cecilia smiled.

"Dante hardly knew Beatrice. He met her twice, I think. And then she was married off to someone else and died young!"

Michael nodded.

"That's true." He thought for a moment, then said, "So you think Shale might go on thinking about Verity and letting the memory bubble inside him for years and years until one day it inspires him to paint great paintings?"

"He might."

"You have a wonderful imagination."

"I know. That's why I'm such a good detective."

THE AUTHOR'S NOTES
AND HIS THANKS

Several people at several times have said to me that in her previous adventures Detective Chief Inspector Cecilia Cavaliere seems to have an unfair advantage as a police detective, since at crucial points in her investigations she invariably receives overt and miraculous divine aid. Looking back over *Siding Star*, *Peacekeeper*, and *Singularity*, I have to admit they have a point. So I decided that in *A Habit of Death*, Cecilia and Verity and their friends would have to work with only that degree of divine aid for which, I trust, all Christians hope at all times: the guidance of the Holy Spirit.

That done, someone else then read through *A Habit of Death* and said they didn't like it so much as the earlier stories because there weren't any supernatural bits in it! All of which, I suppose, goes to show that you can't please everybody. Anyway, *A Habit of Death* is what it is (Wendy told me only this morning that it is cool to say, "it is what it is" — and I had no idea!) and here it is. And being what it is, I trust it still suggests that the universe is a sacrament, even when it appears to be at its most ordinary (whatever that may be), and that we are in divine presence even when we do not notice it — which is, of course, most of the time. In my opinion, Francis Thompson in "The Kingdom of God" got it exactly right:

Does the fish soar to find the ocean,
The eagle plunge to find the air —
That we ask of the stars in motion
If they have rumour of thee there?

Not where the wheeling systems darken,
And our benumbed conceiving soars! —
The drift of pinions, would we hearken,
Beats at our own clay-shuttered doors.

The angels keep their ancient places; —
Turn but a stone, and start a wing!
'Tis ye, 'tis your estrangèd faces,
That miss the many-splendoured thing.

Our modern and perhaps peculiarly western difficulty in "getting" this is, I think, what Sister Chiara was talking about when she spoke to Verity about "left-brain overload," and if anyone doesn't know what she meant, I suggest they might do worse than look at Iain McGilchrist's *The Master and His Emissary* — a remarkable book! After reading it, I feel that I will never be able to think about my perceptions of the world in quite the same way again.

I mentioned in my notes at the end of *Singularity* that I owed the town of Edgestow to C. S. Lewis's *That Hideous Strength,* but should perhaps for form's sake make that acknowledgment here, too. One of the fun things about being a writer of sorts is that you get to borrow all sorts of wonderful things from other people, and provided you admit what you have done, no one seems to mind. And of course, in contrast to most kinds of borrowing, the people you borrow from haven't lost anything, and yet you never have to give it back! How marvelous is that!

Once again, as I close my laptop (when I was young I would have laid aside my pen!) I must say "thank you" to my many conversation partners: first to Wendy Bryan, who continues to put up with my *fiumi di parole*, and then among others to Mishoe Brennecke, Renni Browne, Suzanne Dunstan, Chris Egan, John Gatta, Julia Gatta, Bob Hughes, David Landon, Luann Landon, Rob MacSwain, Sister Madeleine Mary CSM, Susanna Metz, Mary Ann Patterson, Laurie Ramsey, Leslie Richardson, Shannon Roberts, Barbara Stafford, Bill Stafford, and everyone at The Editorial Department. Thank you very much, all of you, for continuing to listen to my questions and to look at my pieces of trivia, thereby indulging me in the enormous pleasure I get from writing them.

Christopher Bryan,
The Epiphany, 2015.

About the Author

Photograph by Wendy Bryan

Sometime Woodward Scholar of Wadham College, Oxford, Christopher Bryan is an Anglican priest, novelist, and academic. He and his wife Wendy live in Sewanee, Tennessee and Exeter, England. His earlier novels are *Siding Star* (Diamond Press, 2012), which was named to Kirkus Reviews Best Books of 2013, *Peacekeeper* (Diamond Press, 2013), and *Singularity* (Diamond Press, 2014): they have been described by author and critic Parker Bauer in *The Weekly Standard* Book Review as "ideal antidotes to the crypto-farces of Dan Brown." Bryan's academic studies include *Listening to the Bible: The Art of Faithful Biblical Interpretation* (Oxford University Press, 2014), *The Resurrection of the Messiah* (Oxford University Press, 2011), the popular *And God Spoke* (Cowley, 2012) (which was among the books chosen as commended reading for the Bishops at the 2008 Lambeth Conference), and *Render to Caesar: Jesus, the Early Church, and the Roman Superpower* (Oxford University Press, 2005).

CPSIA information can be obtained at www.ICGtesting.com
Printed in the USA
LVOW10s0907291115

464530LV00001B/191/P